"Oh, Elaine, Jeff Becker is the most impossible boy I ever met!" Karen burst out. "I hate him!"

"You'd better be careful," Elaine said as they walked. "Carl says that hating somebody is almost the same as loving them."

"That's ridiculous," Karen scoffed.

"I know it sounds contradictory," Elaine admitted, "but when you think about it, it makes sense. The opposite of love isn't hate, it's indifference." She paused. "It's funny how you're always together."

"That's just because he likes to poke fun at me," Karen said, groping for excuses. How, after all these years, after all their battles, could she turn around and admit that, yes, what she and Jeff felt for each other was love? Impossible! Insane!

Or was it?

SENIORS

KISS AND MAKE UP
Created by Eileen Goudge

To Jacqueline Diamond, without whom this book would not be possible

Published by
Dell Publishing Co., Inc.
1 Dag Hammarskjold Plaza
New York, New York 10017

Created by Cloverdale Press
133 Fifth Avenue
New York, New York 10003

Cover photo by Pat Hill

Laurel-Leaf Library ® TM 766734,
Dell Publishing Co., Inc.

Seniors™ is a trademark of Dell Publishing Co., Inc.,
New York, New York.

ISBN: 0-440-94514-3

RL: 6.3

Printed in the United States of America

First printing—January 1986

Chapter One

Even though Karen Waverly had her back turned to the door, she knew immediately that Jeff Becker had entered the civics classroom.

Maybe it was because of the funny way he was walking, brushing each foot along the floor and then thumping it down as if he were some Frankensteinian monster.

Or maybe it was because Gabe Neilsen was going "Psst! Psst!" at Karen to make sure she noticed Jeff. Gabe didn't mean any harm; like the rest of the class, he just enjoyed the fireworks that erupted whenever Karen and Jeff were in the same room.

At any rate, Karen knew he was trying to get her attention, but she pretended not to notice anything. She couldn't help sneaking a look out of the corner of her eye, though. There was something about Jeff that made you want to look at him, she thought, even if he wasn't exactly the movie star type.

For one thing, he had a strong body with wide shoulders—like a football player dressed for a game. Only Jeff's were natural—he didn't need the pads. Then he got really slim down where a guy was supposed to be slim, if you liked the well-built type, that is.

And he had this funny way of looking at you, the light glinting warmly off his blue eyes, that made your bones nearly melt. Anybody's bones—even Karen's, although she would have died rather than admit it.

Jeff was wearing his usual jeans and a torn T-shirt with a patch of tanned shoulder clearly visible through one of the holes. That was what happened when you didn't have a mother, she reflected with an unexpected flush of sympathy. Jeff lived down the street from her family with just his father and their retriever, Bluto.

On the other hand, she reflected, maybe he wore torn clothes on purpose. Sherri Cunningham, who sat at the far side of the room, couldn't seem to take her eyes off that exposed patch of shoulder.

He stopped to talk to one of his friends at the back of the room. If only he'd stay there! Karen shifted uneasily in her seat, wishing that, today of all days, Jeff would have called in sick with the potato famine or something—he never came down with anything ordinary.

Today she was scheduled to give an oral report, and she'd worked hard on her presentation. The subject was civil disobedience—something Karen hadn't known much about, but her mother had helped by talking about the civil rights marches of

2

her younger days.

Karen's palms were beginning to prickle. Ugh. Sweat. It always happened when she got nervous. She could imagine how Jeff would tease her about getting sweaty palms over a stupid report.

But it wasn't a stupid report! She really wanted to do well today. She'd always maintained a solid B average, even though she realized she could probably do better, but in the past, grades had never seemed very important.

But watching her brother Fred cram for his premed classes had started Karen thinking. She'd begun to realize that it wasn't enough anymore just to slide by. Something else bothered her, too.

Karen looked up. Maybe it was fate, but she found herself staring right at Emma Greenway—quiet, studious Emma Greenway, who was now class treasurer, even though she could hardly balance a checkbook.

When the last class treasurer, Mary Willis, moved to Sacramento two months ago, Karen had gotten up her nerve to run for the position. After all, she was interested in accounting and wanted to get a job in business someday.

When Emma ran against her, Karen figured it was no contest. Most of the kids didn't even know who Emma was, whereas everybody knew Karen. She was their favorite public speaker, the one who joked about running off to Mexico with the treasury. But Karen had also believed that in spite of her wisecracking, she genuinely *wanted* to be treasurer.

Instead, the kids had voted overwhelmingly for Emma. Apparently they'd thought that earnest, diligent, reliable Emma would take the job more seriously than Karen, who, obviously, was running just for fun. After the results were announced, Karen had thought her jaw would crack from smiling and pretending she didn't care, when all she really wanted to do was pound on the furniture and cry.

Well, she'd learned her lesson. She wasn't going to louse things up for herself anymore by goofing off when she should be acting like, well, like Emma Greenway.

"Hey, Red," Jeff announced loudly enough for everyone to hear as he plopped into the chair next to Karen. He shot her a mischievous grin, blue eyes sparkling beneath a thatch of shaggy blond hair. Karen felt her annoyance flare — why was he always calling attention to her red hair, like she was some kind of freak?

If her best friend, Betsy Simmons, hadn't moved away last semester, the chair wouldn't have been vacant. But now Jeff was sitting there waiting for a reply. So was the rest of the class, judging by the way their conversations had died.

Karen turned toward him. "Well, if it isn't Bloopers, Blunders, and Practical Jokes in person. Hey, what do you get if you cross Jeff Becker with a groundhog?"

"Um — I give up," he said cheerfully. "What?"

"Six more weeks of insults!" she shot back.

Across the room, Elaine Gregory gave her the thumbs-up signal. The gesture of approval, coming from Elaine whom Karen liked and respected, made her feel a little better. Maybe she could even change her image, as Elaine had recently done.

Just a few months ago, Elaine had swapped her tortoiseshell glasses for contact lenses, restyled her shoulder-length brown hair, and turned herself into a knockout. And she was still one of the best students in the senior class.

Elaine's makeover was just the kind of thing Karen needed to get ready for next year, when she planned to study business at Columbia Junior College.

Maybe Elaine would be willing to give her a few tips: for starters, what to do with Karen's frizzy reddish-gold hair. Her mother said it reminded her of a halo, but Karen thought it looked more like a clown wig. If she could figure out how to appear more sophisticated, maybe even Jeff Becker would finally treat her with respect.

But he obviously wasn't about to start now.

"I always feel safe sitting next to you," he quipped. "Since your mom's a veterinarian, I figure you must have had your shots."

To her relief, the teacher, Ms. O'Neill, walked in from the hall, and the class came to order.

Ms. O'Neill, a short, chunky woman with a no-nonsense approach to teaching, recapped the chapter they'd been assigned to read over the weekend. As usual, she threw out questions that caught a few students off guard.

But then she called on Elaine, who explained promptly and clearly the reasons for the freedom of speech and freedom of assembly provisions in the Bill of Rights. Karen smiled her approval and was pleased when Elaine smiled back.

"Karen Waverly, are you ready with your report?" Ms. O'Neill asked.

Karen felt her heart skip a beat. *This was it.* "Yes, I am," she announced, picking up her papers and walking to the head of the class.

"I'm going to talk about civil disobedience," she said, feeling a little shaky. Then, clearing her throat, she launched into her talk. Karen tried to concentrate on her notes, but it was disconcerting to stand up in front facing everybody. You noticed all sorts of things—notes being passed, people doodling, jaws moving slowly on forbidden wads of gum...Just when Karen was starting to relax, she noticed that Jeff was acting peculiarly. Jeff was chewing on something, but she couldn't tell what it was.

"Civil disobedience is when you break the law in a nonviolent way to uphold a principle," Karen explained. She spoke quickly to hide her nervousness and went on to explain about the sit-in of the sixties. But all the while, her attention kept returning to Jeff.

What on earth could he be chomping on? she wondered, fascinated yet revolted by his exaggerated motions. Jeff's jaw was waggling from side to side. He looked like a cow munching on its cud.

"Um...the early suffragettes used civil disobedience to, er, protest the laws that kept women from voting."

Struggle as she might, Karen's gaze kept returning to Jeff's face. He was rolling his eyes and puffing out his cheeks as if trying to blow a bubble. At any moment, a pink orb would appear. She could imagine it growing bigger and bigger. Was he planning to pop it in the middle of her talk?

She forced herself to concentrate. "The—uh—

modern idea of disobedience owes a lot to Mahatma Gandhi, who helped India win its independence from Great Britain, and also to Dr. Martin Luther King, Jr. . . . "

Jeff contorted his face hideously, and suddenly she realized that he wasn't chewing on anything. He was making it up just to distract her.

She couldn't remember what she meant to say next. Ms. O'Neill, sitting in the back of the room, frowned and tapped her fingernails on the wooden arm of her chair.

Just as Karen was wishing the floor would open up and swallow her, her mother's final words flooded back. With relief, she quickly finished her speech. "You, um, have to think carefully before using civil disobedience, because even though you believe you're doing the right thing, you're still breaking the law."

"Thank you, Karen." Ms. O'Neill stood up, and Karen stumbled unhappily back to her seat.

She refused to look at Jeff, even though she could feel his eyes on her as she slid into her chair. She'd worked so hard on her talk, and Jeff had wrecked it! The teacher probably thought she'd hardly spent any time on it at all.

Ms. O'Neill was asking the class for examples of civil disobedience. Karen wondered if cracking Jeff over the head with a ruler would qualify. She'd never figure him out, not if she lived forever. He'd been teasing her since the second grade, when Karen and her family had moved into the neighborhood.

Nervous and shy the first day at her new school, she'd sat by herself to eat lunch. She could still remember opening her lunch box and seeing a huge, hideous potato bug crawling across her Thermos.

Karen had shrieked and then, seeing the delighted grin on Jeff's face, immediately figured out that he was the one who'd put it there. Furious, Karen had dumped the lunch box over his head, and the bug had ended up crawling down Jeff's shirt.

Ever since then, her ongoing squabbles with Jeff had provided entertainment for the rest of their classmates. Sometimes Karen felt as if she were a prisoner stuck behind a grinning comedy mask.

The bell rang, jolting her out of her thoughts. Grabbing her books, Karen headed to the front of the class, where Ms. O'Neill stood.

"I wanted to apologize about my talk," Karen began. "I really did work hard on it, and I'm sorry I blew it."

The teacher shook her head reassuringly. "Don't feel bad, Karen. You did a fine job. A lot of people get rattled when they have to talk in front of a group. That's one reason I assign oral reports—so you'll get some practice in public speaking."

"Thanks, Ms. O'Neill." As she turned away, Karen ran right into Jeff.

"Hey, Karen, I'm sorry if I messed up your speech," he said. He looked so contrite, she almost believed it. Then he ruined it all by adding, "Hey, you know, you're cute when you're mad."

Karen stalked away, even more furious at Jeff than before. "How's it going with your not-so-secret admirer?" Elaine fell into step beside Karen at the doorway, her brown eyes twinkling.

"My *what*?" Karen asked, nearly dropping her

load of books. "You don't mean *Jeff*. He hates my guts."

Elaine laughed. "Sure, that's why he's always looking at you and teasing you. He hates you so much, he can't leave you alone."

Karen stared at her, wondering if Elaine had gone crazy. "And I always thought you were the smart one," she said, laughing.

They walked to their lockers together, Karen hurrying to keep up with long-legged Elaine. At five feet three, Karen would have given anything for just a few more inches. A slim, rather angular figure emerged from the crowd. It was Carl Schmidt, Elaine's boyfriend.

"Hi." He included them both in his nod.

"Oh, Carl, I was looking for you," Elaine said. "What time did you want to make our study date tonight?"

Carl pushed aside a stray lock of sandy-brown hair. He had a thin, serious face, and Karen almost giggled when she thought how much he already looked like the psychiatrist he wanted to be.

"That's what I wanted to talk to you about," he said. "My brother's run into a big problem with a computer program, and he asked me to help him out."

"Too bad it isn't video games," Karen broke in. "Those are Jeff's specialty." Then she wanted to bite her tongue. She'd better be careful or she'd give people the impression she actually cared about Jeff's interests.

Elaine was staring at Carl with an expression somewhere between exasperation and disbelief.

"You're breaking our date because your brother needs help programming his computer? Is it that urgent?"

Carl shrugged. "You know, it really drives you crazy when you hit a stumbling block like that. It would be an act of cruelty to make him wait until tomorrow night—and anyway, he's got a date then."

"Well, we certainly wouldn't want to make him break it!" Elaine replied, then softened. "I'm sorry, Carl. I know we were just getting together to study."

"We're still on for Saturday! And we've got a Wildcat meeting after school Wednesday," Carl said, referring to the yearbook committee that he and Elaine were on together. "Maybe we can go for ice cream afterwards."

"Yeah, sure." Elaine managed a weak smile as Carl walked away.

"Guys can really drive you crazy," Karen sighed.

"Yeah." Elaine banged her books onto the shelf in her locker. " 'Drive you crazy' is right. You know what? I studied like crazy yesterday so I wouldn't have to concentrate on anything but Carl during our 'study date,' and now I've got a whole Monday night free with nothing to do."

An idea popped into Karen's head. "Do you like old movies?" she asked Elaine. "My brother Zack taped *The Maltese Falcon*—I was going to watch it tonight. Do you want to come over and watch it, too? We could make popcorn—if you don't mind wading through brothers and pets. Our house is full of them."

"Hey, that sounds great," Elaine replied. "Your house must be like mine—we've got a dog, a cat, two hamsters, and my three younger sisters. Sometimes I feel like Dr. Dolittle."

They settled on the time, and Karen gave Elaine directions for getting there. A bubble of excitement welled up in Karen as they parted. Since Betsy had moved away, she hadn't had a close friend. Already, she felt comfortable with Elaine. It would be fun to get to know her brainy classmate better.

Her plans for the evening almost made up for having Jeff Becker spoil her report. Maybe Elaine could even help her figure out how to make Jeff stop teasing her.

Remembering what Elaine had said about her "not-so-secret admirer," Karen felt her face grow warm. Could Jeff really think of her in that way? Flustered, she stopped in the middle of the hallway. Part of her was excited by the idea, the other part uncertain. Would she like that if it were true? If she and Jeff were to become . . .

Nonsense! What was she even thinking? She and Jeff were confirmed adversaries. They couldn't get along as a couple if they were the last people on earth. Elaine might have a straight-A average, but she didn't know everything. And this time, she was dead wrong.

Feeling a little more like herself, Karen continued on down the hall. She thought about the way Sherri had stared at the hole in Jeff's shirt. There was certainly no accounting for taste.

Chapter Two

The bus ride home from school didn't seem to take as long as usual, maybe because Karen was buoyed by the anticipation of seeing Elaine that night.

She'd even hoped they might sit together on the bus, but Elaine had ridden her bike to school that day. It was the first time Karen had admitted to herself just how lonely she'd been since Betsy left.

Oh, sure, she had plenty of casual friends, and boys asked her out fairly often, but nobody seemed to stick. It was a little like trying to play chords on a piano when you didn't know what you were doing, she decided. You had to hit a lot of wrong notes before you found the ones that sounded good together.

Of course, sometimes she had Jeff for an uninvited seatmate on the bus, but he usually kept up a steady barrage of teasing, to the delight of their fellow riders. Karen thought of it as a sort of verbal tennis match, and she couldn't help enjoying it when she managed to annihilate him with a zinger or two of her own.

Today, however, Jeff was wrapped up in talking to a couple of his friends about a new video game called Killer Space Monsters. He didn't seem to notice her, and she found herself growing annoyed, first at Jeff, then at herself. Why should she care if Jeff was ignoring her? Isn't that exactly what she wanted? She purposely ignored him as she stepped off the bus at her stop. Jeff's house was located near the next stop, but he sometimes got off at her stop rather than end their teasing match. Today he didn't. Well, he could fall off the face of the earth, for all she cared!

The Waverlys' house was a rambling two-story structure, its clapboard surface half-hidden beneath climbing roses. The yard itself, a favorite digging spot for neighborhood dogs and cats, showed more bare patches than grass.

She remembered when her parents had bought the place ten years before, back when her dad was still alive. The family had moved from San Francisco to Glenwood because Karen's mom, Anne Waverly, had been invited to go into partnership in an animal clinic with an old family friend, Art Brenner. It was Art who'd encouraged her to be a veterinarian in the first place, and the opportunity was too good to pass up. Fortunately, her father, a lawyer, didn't mind commuting back to his office in San Francisco each day.

As she walked up the broad wooden steps to the front door, Karen absentmindedly bent to pat her orange-striped cat, Garfield. He meowed contentedly and rubbed against her ankle.

Pushing open the door, Karen wondered with a pang what their lives would have been like if her father hadn't died.

She decided, as she stepped inside, that the worn carpet would probably have been replaced, since her father had made good money as a lawyer. And they might have bought new furniture instead of keeping the old couch and chairs, which were covered with scratches from a series of pets.

Although it was hard to imagine a pleasanter home or a more loving family, Karen still missed her father. He'd died a year and a half after they'd moved — when she was nine. Remembering his wise brown eyes, the scent of the pipe he'd smoked, and the way they'd read aloud together from the Sunday comics, Karen felt the familiar lump in her throat.

The only things that stuck in her mind about that awful day were the chilled silence that filled their house and the words *heart attack* that kept echoing in her head when her oldest brother, Fred, only two years older than she was, had handed her the phone. Their mother was on the other end, at the hospital where they'd brought her dad.

Karen admired the way her mother had coped since then. Anne Waverly had somehow managed to support three young children as well as an endless stream of animals.

Still, Karen admitted to herself, sometimes she thought she'd get more attention if she turned into a dog with a broken paw. There was never enough time to sit and talk with her mother, especially now that the business was booming. Neither Anne nor Art could bear to turn away an animal in pain, however, even if the owner couldn't afford to pay. As a result, the Waverly family ate a lot of spaghetti dinners, and Karen sewed most of her own clothes.

In a way, that was why she'd gotten so interested in business. The clinic's books were always a mess, and Karen had taken a summer course in bookkeeping so she could handle them.

Anne had finally decided it was too much work for a high school student, and now she and Art used a bank service. But she'd allowed Karen to take over the family's own ledgers. It was fun, entering income and expenses in columns and seeing it all balance neatly at the end of the month—except when they ran into unexpected stuff like the washing machine breaking down. But Zack and Fred had gotten pretty handy at fixing things like that.

Now that both her brothers were attending Columbia Junior College—Zack was studying filmmaking, and Fred had enrolled in premed courses—Karen was trying to help more in the house and clinic, in addition to doing the bookkeeping. And as a result her mother had begun treating her more like an adult.

Tweety, the parakeet, chirped loudly, rousing Karen out of her reverie. She glanced over at his cage which hung in a corner of the living room safely away from marauding cats.

Afternoon sunlight filtered through the dark red curtains, casting a ruby glow over everything. The house might be shabby, but it was certainly welcoming, Karen thought with a burst of pride. "Hi, Tweets," she said, walking over and pushing a sunflower seed through the bars.

After dashing upstairs to drop off her books, she retreated to the kitchen and began scrubbing potatoes for dinner.

A few minutes later, the thrum of an aging automobile engine in the driveway followed by a clattering in the front hall announced that her brothers were home.

Fred ambled into the kitchen. "Need any help?" he asked.

"Sure. You could cut up the potatoes while I get the chicken ready." Karen wiped her hands on her apron. "I'm having a girl friend over tonight. You weren't planning to use the video, were you?"

"No, I've got a lecture." Fred's tall, gaunt figure towered over her as he picked up the kitchen knife. "Dinner will be ready by six o'clock, won't it? I've got to leave by six thirty."

"Sure." Karen couldn't help noticing how sunken his cheeks had become. Fred had been studying hard this year, maybe too hard. He was only nineteen, but already his eyes looked tired around the edges. He seemed nothing like the devil-may-care boy he'd been until last summer.

Karen could remember when Fred thought about hardly anything but surfing and going out with his girl friend Kathy. They'd been planning to get married—until she dropped him suddenly and eloped with a man she'd just met.

After that, Fred had buckled down to his studies, and his grades had shot up; but she worried about him, and she knew her mother did, too.

"How's it going?" Zack ambled in, giving Karen a playful squeeze. Nobody would ever have to worry about him, she thought. Brawny and handsome with merry blue eyes and thick brown hair that had a mind of its own, Zack made friends easily and met life with zest. Bright and creative, he made good grades, too, but rarely allowed his studies to interfere with his social life—unless he was involved in a special film project. Film was both his passion and his major in college.

"You get to make the salad." She steered him in the direction of the refrigerator.

"Sure." Zack proceeded to pull out not only the lettuce and tomatoes but also a bag of marshmallows and a jar of nuts. "I can really do something with this."

"Our stomachs aren't made out of cast iron," Karen warned. She glanced at Fred for support, but he was staring fixedly at the potatoes as he diced them, his thoughts a million miles away.

"Hey, did you ever see that short film Alan Arkin made about his two sons cooking up a mess in the kitchen?" Zack asked as he tossed his unlikely ingredients together.

Zack thought of everything in terms of film. He always had, but now that he was eighteen and actually making student films in college, he'd gotten worse than ever.

"Oh, that reminds me," Karen said, "is it okay if I watch *The Maltese Falcon* tonight? A girl friend of mine is coming over."

"Fine with me," Zack said. "Is she cute?"

"None of your business," Karen teased back.

Within a few minutes, the chicken was in the oven, the potatoes boiling on the stove, and the salad stowed in the refrigerator. Alone in the kitchen, Karen fixed a pot of coffee for her mother.

Perfect timing. With a hiss and a grind, the Waverlys' second old clunker halted in the driveway.

"Hi, everybody!" Anne called. From the kitchen, Karen could follow her mother's progress—an exchange of chirps with Tweety, the rattling of Doggone the mongrel's collar as Anne played with him, and finally the light tap of footsteps coming down the hall.

"Hi," Karen said.

"You've even got my coffee ready! Thanks." Anne went right to the pot and poured herself a cup.

She looked tousled, as usual, at the end of a long day. Her dark auburn hair was escaping in tendrils from its knot, but her green eyes—the same color as Karen's—danced with even more mischief than usual.

Anne hardly ever wore makeup, and her wardrobe consisted mostly of slacks and blouses that could be tossed in the washing machine after a tough day among the animals. Even so, she managed to look great. Karen wished as many heads turned for her when *she* walked down the street as they did for her mom.

Anne dated fairly often, but none of the men seemed to matter much. Like mother, like daughter, Karen thought.

"What have you been up to?" Joining her mother at the kitchen table, Karen relished this moment of togetherness. It was one of the reasons she'd started getting dinner ready herself, so Anne would have time to relax with her. "Busy day?"

18

"Busy enough, but no rabbits," her mother said, and they both chuckled.

It was an old joke with them. One day Anne had been examining a pregnant rabbit when it gave birth right there in the clinic. "As if we weren't busy enough!" Anne had exclaimed later. "The patients multiply right there in the operating room!"

Now, as her mother ran through the events of the day, Karen couldn't help noticing how young and happy she looked. What on earth could have caused it?

"And then, just as I was getting ready to leave, who do you think came into the clinic?" Anne said.

"The entire Barnum and Bailey Circus?"

"No!" Her mother chuckled. "No, it was Albert Becker. You know, Bluto — the golden retriever — he'd been in some kind of fight with another dog, and I think he got the worst of it."

Karen felt confused. Bluto was Jeff's dog. Her mother had known the Beckers for years. Why should she make such a fuss about Mr. Becker coming into the clinic?

"After I patched Bluto up," Anne continued blithely, "Albert and I got to talking. He's a very interesting man, you know." She wore a dreamy look Karen didn't like.

"He is?"

"He loves exotic animals." Anne got up and fetched some carrot sticks from the refrigerator. "He said he's always wanted to go on a photo safari in Africa. Doesn't that sound facinating?"

"Yes, I guess so." Although she didn't really like coffee, Karen fixed herself a cup just to have something to do, adding lots of cream and sugar to kill the taste. She didn't like what she was hearing, not one bit.

She'd never paid much attention to Jeff's father. He was someone in the background, a rather solemn man who wore glasses and was about Jeff's height—not really tall, but a lot taller than Karen. Now she tried to picture him through her mom's eyes. Was he handsome? Was he the kind of man Mom would want to go out with?

"We have a surprising amount in common," her mother was saying. "I always knew he was a single parent, of course—he and his wife were divorced when Jeff and his sister were very young. But we've both been so wrapped up in raising our children and in our careers that we've never really had more than a nodding acquaintance. His situation is unusual: he and his wife split the children—Mrs. Becker got the girl, and Albert got the boy. Isn't that odd? But I suppose it makes sense."

"Yeah, if Mr. Becker likes exotic animals, I can see why he'd want Jeff," Karen said.

"Oh, Karen!" Anne laughed, then rested her chin on the heel of her hand. "Isn't it amazing how you can live down the street from somebody for ten years and never really know him?"

Before Karen could figure out what to say, Fred poked into the kitchen to see if dinner was ready, and in the commotion that followed Karen lost any chance to find out more about her mother and Mr. Becker.

Surely Anne couldn't be interested in him as a...well, seriously, that is. At the prospect of her mother falling for Jeff's father Karen felt a tingling that she was sure meant her blood was running cold. Then an even more horrifying thought hit her. What if they got married? Then she'd have *Jeff* for a stepbrother!

She could just see it. Jeff living here in her house. She'd walk into the bathroom and find him standing there in his underwear, grinning at her and flexing his big shoulders. (Could guys really flex their shoulders? Well, knowing him, he'd figure out a way.)

Maybe he'd pop into her room while she was dressing for a date. Karen usually didn't bother to lock her door, and Jeff would probably think it was funny, walking in and catching her in her slip. Or worse.

It was an absolute nightmare. Enough to make Cyndi Lauper's hair turn gray.

She tried to join in the conversation during dinner. There was no point in making a big deal out of this; it would probably come to nothing, she told herself, not really believing it. After all, hadn't Mom just poured salt in her coffee instead of sugar? That meant she was daydreaming—about Jeff's father, probably.

Later, as Karen was setting up the popcorn maker, Anne poked her head into the den and asked, "Do you think I should get a new dress? He asked me out for Friday night."

"Uh...that's up to you, Mom," Karen mumbled, ducking her head and pretending to be busy with the VCR until her mother had gone.

A date! Sure, Anne had dated plenty of men, but she never worried about what she wore. Come to

21

think of it, she hardly ever mentioned the guys at all. Certainly she didn't get excited and flustered about them, not like this.

What if Anne really liked Mr. Becker? What if they started holding hands and kissing good night? What if . . .

The doorbell rang, and Karen hurried to answer it.

Elaine was wearing a scarf and carrying an umbrella. "Hi," she said, stepping inside.

"Is it raining?" Karen asked.

"No, but it looks like it might."

"If it does, I'll drive you home," Karen promised. She wished she had as much foresight as Elaine. Half the time, Karen never noticed the weather until it was too late and she was either soaked or freezing.

They talked about school while they fixed popcorn. Fred had left for his lecture half an hour earlier, and Karen knew her mother was upstairs, probably reading a zoology magazine.

That left Zack unaccounted for, but not for long. Soon after the movie started, he wandered into the den, pretending he'd lost a book but actually, Karen suspected, wanting to get a look at her friend.

She stopped the tape and introduced them, hoping Zack would promptly disappear, but he didn't.

"You're interested in films?" he asked.

"That's right," Elaine said. "Alfred Hitchcock is one of my favorites." To Karen's astonishment, Zack sat down and helped himself to some of their popcorn. "He's a master of the art. Have you seen *Psycho*?"

"Not more than two or three times," Elaine

quipped. She leaned forward in her chair, her eyes fixed on Zack.

"I suppose you realize that he never shows the knife and the woman in the shower at the same time?" Zack continued, warming to the subject. "That's a brilliant job of editing, making the audience believe it's witnessing a horrible bloody murder without actually showing anything."

"And of course you know he used chocolate for the blood," Elaine replied, clearly fascinated.

"And stand-ins for both Janet Leigh and Anthony Perkins," Zack said.

They were off, both absorbed in their subject. Karen, watching curiously from the couch, couldn't help noticing the zing of electricity that passed between Elaine and Zack every time they looked at each other. Her amazement grew. Ten minutes later, the two were practically fighting over how many different editing cuts Hitchcock had made in one minute of film. Finally, Zack suggested that they look up the answer in one of his film books, and they darted upstairs to Zack's room.

Karen started another batch of popcorn, and a minute later Elaine came down alone and told her the answer was seventy-eight. She also wore a dreamy look, much like Anne's. What's going on around here? Karen wondered. Is it something in the water?

Settling down, they watched the movie together in easy companionship.

Afterwards, the girls sat in the den talking and sipping diet sodas.

"Something weird happened this afternoon,"

Karen said. She wanted Elaine's advice and tried to think of the right way to phrase her problem. "My mother seems to be interested in a man—not that she hasn't dated a few times, but, well, this is different."

"Serious?" Elaine asked.

"It is for me!" Karen made a face. "He's Jeff Becker's father."

"No kidding!"

"I mean, they just live down the street, so it isn't the first time he and my mother have met, but... What if they start going together? It would be awful!"

"Oh, I don't know." Elaine nibbled at a half-popped kernel from the bottom of the bowl. "You and your mom could double-date with Jeff and his father."

Karen groaned.

"Sure, he can be kind of obnoxious, but guys are that way in high school. Girls always mature faster than boys," Elaine said, and Karen smiled. "Look at Carl. What kind of guy breaks a date with his girl friend because his brother's stuck on a computer program? But my mother says they grow out of it when they get older."

"You think maybe Jeff will shed his skin like a snake and turn out to be Tom Selleck?" Karen joked.

"Actually, I think he's kind of cute now." Elaine swallowed the last of her soft drink.

"You do?" Karen thought about Sherri Cunningham again. There was a funny feeling in the pit of her stomach. Not that she cared if other girls flirted with Jeff...

The unexpected patter of rain against the windows interrupted them. "I'll drive you home," Karen offered.

"Boy, I'd really appreciate it," Elaine said, looking out into the darkness.

On the drive to Elaine's, Karen felt a flush of happiness when her new friend turned to her and said impulsively, "I'm really glad you invited me over tonight. I'd been wanting to get to know you better, but you and Betsy were always so close."

"I thought you were too busy—I mean, you're so tight with Alex and Kit and Lori." Karen had sometimes watched the four girls, envying their obvious closeness.

"That doesn't mean I don't like other people, too." They reached Elaine's house, and she climbed out, opening her umbrella. "I'll see you tomorrow."

"Bye!" Karen called. After watching to make sure Elaine got inside safely, she drove slowly home. The rain gave her a lonely, hollow feeling, and the words to a song ran through her head: "The times, they are a-changin'..."

Changes. She thought of her mother, talking animatedly about Mr. Becker; of Fred and Kathy, now a couple only in old photographs; of her own upcoming graduation from high school; Jeff as he'd looked a few years ago, one summer at the beach...

She shook her head to wipe away the images.

At home, with uncharacteristic generosity, Zack had washed the popcorn bowl and straightened the den.

"I waited up to make sure you got home all right," he said when she came in.

Karen eyed him dubiously. "Oh?"

"And, uh"—Zack tried to look casual but failed—"I wondered if you'd mind giving me the phone number of your cute friend. Elaine, isn't that her name?"

"Aren't you dating somebody at school?" she asked.

"That's pretty much over with." Zack grinned. "I mean, you can't expect a guy to do without female companionship." He pulled an honest-to-goodness little black book out of his pocket, along with the Mark Cross pen Karen had given him for Christmas. He stood there with the pen poised, watching her expectantly.

Karen hesitated. She didn't want to put Elaine in an awkward position. "She's already got a boyfriend."

He shrugged. "They're not engaged, are they?"

"No, but she's really crazy about Carl," she hedged.

"But I'm such an irresistible guy," Zack teased. "Women can't resist filmmakers. Look at Warren Beatty. Look at Robert Redford."

"Look at Woody Allen," Karen pointed out.

"I always thought he was kind of cute." Zack mugged. "Hey, come on, I'm getting writer's cramp just standing here. Elaine can always tell me to buzz off. Besides, I just want to talk to her."

"Oh, all right." Karen looked up the number in her school directory and gave it to him.

Afterwards, as she got ready for bed, Karen wondered what kind of boyfriend Zack would make. Probably lots of fun, but you'd have to have a quick mind to keep up with him—like Elaine, only Elaine wouldn't be interested, since she had Carl. Or would

she? Karen recalled the way Elaine had l[...]
Zack, her dreamy expression after she'd gon[...]
his room.

Karen tried to picture Jeff Becker ever being any
body's boyfriend, and couldn't. He'd probably put a
whoopee cushion on the car seat before picking a
girl up for the senior prom.

Surely his father couldn't be all that much better,
Karen tried to reassure herself. Anne would get tired
of him in no time.

She wished she felt more certain about that.

Chapter Three

The sky was overcast the next morning, which didn't help Karen's gray mood.

When the school bus pulled up, she saw that Elaine was already sharing a seat with Kit. They both waved warmly as Karen climbed inside, and she waved back.

Kit fascinated Karen. She was a real knockout, without even trying. With her tumble of wheat-colored hair, Christie Brinkley body, and exuberant good spirits, she seemed to light up any room—including the interior of the school bus—that she walked into.

On top of that, Kit was probably the best dancer ever to whirl through a Glenwood ballet studio. And yet she was one of the kindest people Karen had ever met.

Last year, when Karen was stuck in the hospital after an appendectomy, Kit had dropped in with a book of crossword puzzles and a copy of *Mad* zine to cheer her up, even though they hardly ᴋ each other.

The seats near Elaine and Kit were taken, so Karen found a place near the back of the bus. Then, just as it was about to depart, the doors whooshed open again and Jeff clambered inside. Karen's heart somersaulted. She recalled Elaine's comment. Yes, he really *was* cute. She could never have admitted anything like that out loud, though. Especially not to Jeff—then his head would be twice as swelled.

His eyes searched the length of the bus and stopped at Karen. Strangely, she was torn between happiness and dismay when he headed straight for her and slid into the empty seat at her side.

She braced herself for the inevitable insults. Usually he turned himself inside out trying to provoke a response.

But today, oddly enough, he didn't say anything, just stared into space as the bus rumbled on its way.

He was dressed differently, too, although that might be because of the cool weather. Instead of a torn T-shirt under his Windbreaker, he was wearing a new-looking blue sweat shirt that didn't even have a slogan on it.

It felt funny, sitting there next to Jeff, not saying anything. Some of the other kids waited expectantly for a minute, then lost interest.

Once the bus jostled them together. For some reason, the momentary thud of his body against hers made Karen's knees feel spongy.

"Did your mom say anything to you?" Jeff asked finally in a low voice.

"She said she ran into your dad," Karen admitted. "They've got a date Friday night."

"Yeah, she said something about it." Karen gazed out the window, trying to act as if she were more interested in the view than in her mother's romance. But Burt Reynolds could have run down the middle of Glenwood in his undershorts that morning, and she wouldn't have noticed.

"You'd think they were old enough to be past that sort of stuff," Jeff grumbled.

"My mother's only forty-two," Karen couldn't resist answering. "She won't be collecting social security for a few years yet."

"You mean you think it's a good idea, the two of them going out?" Jeff's blue eyes were full of disbelief.

"No, I didn't mean that." Karen tried to find the right words. "I think my mother has a right to date, but it could be really awkward if she and your father got serious."

The bus stopped, and some freshmen got on, hooting and calling to one another as they scrambled for seats. Several of them glanced at Jeff. He usually kidded with them and swapped tips on the latest games at the video arcade—but today he didn't even notice them.

"I really hated it when my parents got divorced." Jeff seemed to be talking to himself. "I worried about Dad all the time, because he's the type to take everything real seriously. Isn't that funny? They always talk about how the kids need to adjust, but I think he had a harder time with the divorce than I did."

30

Joking and teasing had always appeared to be a natural part of Jeff's personality. Now Karen wondered if he'd purposely developed it as a way of cheering up his father.

"My mom's really a nice person." Karen tried to reassure him. "I know she'd never hurt your dad."

The sympathy in her voice had the opposite effect of what she'd intended. Instead of opening up more, Jeff blinked hard, as if awakening from a daze.

The dark depths she'd glimpsed vanished from his eyes. "I don't know what I'm worrying about." He grinned. "If your mother's as argumentative as you, Dad won't be dating her for long."

Karen prickled, but at least now she felt as if she were on familiar ground. "Yeah, well, if your father's anything like you, he probably just asked her out because he wants to get out of paying the vet bill," she shot back, gaining a point in her favor.

In a lot of ways, sparring with Jeff was easier than taking him seriously, she thought. When he was teasing her, she forgot what a nice person he could be when he wanted to. She didn't have a chance to get carried away by romantic feelings....

Unwillingly, Karen found herself remembering an incident from two years ago, the summer they were sophomores.

She'd gone to spend a week with her aunt Ellen, who lived right on the beach a couple of hours' drive south of Glenwood.

What a shock it was to learn that the cottage where Jeff and his father spent two weeks every summer was located only a few blocks away! The town was a small one, and they kept running into

31

each other. Without the other kids around to egg him on, Jeff had been much more relaxed than usual, and she'd noticed new things about him.

For instance, he'd begun to lose that beanpole boyish look, and Karen had realized with surprise that he was going to be handsome when he grew up. She'd also discovered that summer that when he wanted to be nice, Jeff could charm the sea gulls out of the sky.

They'd played volleyball with other teenagers they met on the beach and shared a bonfire with a group of families one night.

To her surprise, Karen had found herself growing more and more attracted to Jeff. She'd dreamed about what it would be like to kiss him. He and his father stayed on at the beach after she went home; but it wasn't long before school would start, and Karen had looked forward eagerly to seeing him again.

Glenwood High held a mixer dance the first Saturday night after classes started. Karen was sure Jeff would spend the evening with her, letting everyone at school see how they felt about each other.

She sewed a new dress in a light green color that brought out her eyes. Even her brothers had noticed her preoccupation and started to tease her about it.

Then that night Karen walked in and saw Jeff dancing with Meredith Shaw, a new girl at Glenwood High.

Meredith was pretty, with a china doll face and a way of fluttering her eyelids at boys. It made Karen want to throw up, but Jeff seemed to love it. Her dream of romance crumbled before her eyes that night as she watched Jeff spend the whole evening with Meredith. He took her out several times after that, too, Karen knew.

Karen felt as if she were walking around with a chest full of broken glass for weeks afterwards. It hurt every time she thought about Jeff.

After that, to show him she didn't care, she made some flippant remarks about his dating activities— especially when he picked up some freshman named Jeannie, whom he dated off and on for the rest of the semester. Jeff retaliated with remarks of his own, and they were off and running.

And that's how it had been ever since. Karen was jerked from her thoughts as the bus hissed to a stop. Quickly she scrambled ahead of Jeff, wanting to put as much distance between the two of them as possible.

The rest of the day wasn't much of an improvement. It was hard to keep her attention focused on her classes when she had so many worries buzzing around in her head.

To make matters worse, she had a meeting of the Community Service Committee after school, which Jeff served on also. Karen thought about skipping it, but she really cared about the committee's work.

It had been set up because a lot of the students, including Karen and Jeff, wanted to share some of their own good fortune. They were always reading in the newspaper about people who had terrible things happen to them. At first, the committee had talked about raising money for hungry people overseas, but then they'd decided to stick closer to home.

Their latest project was to help raise money for

heart surgery for a five-year-old boy who lived in Glenwood. Some of the adult service clubs in town were also contributing, and the committee hoped to bring in at least several hundred more dollars to the fund.

They met in the civics classroom after school with Ms. O'Neill, who was the committee's adviser. Everyone arrived slightly damp from the drizzling rain.

The topic of the day was how to raise money.

"Maybe we could have a car wash," suggested Gayle Rodgers, one of the committee members.

"In the rain?" Jeff commented.

"Please don't suggest selling magazine subscriptions," moaned Ben Davidson. "My neighbors have signs saying NO SOLICITING stuck up all over the place."

"Maybe we could show a film during lunch hour about heart operations, and everybody would want to help out," said Christina Farrel.

"Or they might throw up their lunches from all the blood and gore," Karen couldn't resist commenting.

"I've got it!" Jeff crowed. "We'll have a contest— we can make it Heart Attack! The guy who contributes the least money has to take Karen out on a date."

Karen felt her face redden as the others laughed.

Ms. O'Neill got the discussion back on track, and finally Gayle came up with the idea of an after-school carnival.

"It doesn't have to be real elaborate," she said.

"I could bring my computer over," Jeff offered. "I've got lots of video games. Maybe I could give lessons in how to play—the underclassmen would really like that."

Karen was searching for an idea of her own when she heard Jeff say, "Wouldn't Karen make a great Gypsy fortune-teller? With all that bushy hair, she'd really look authentic." Outraged, Karen could scarcely control her anger. She wanted more than anything to strangle Jeff with her bare hands. But before she could reply with a caustic remark of her own, Christina spoke up.

"Oh, I think she'd be cute. Karen, you could make up funny fortunes!"

"I don't really know anything about fortune-telling," she said quickly. "I could be the cashier."

Gayle chuckled. "Yeah, and run off to Mexico? We know about you and money!"

Karen groaned inwardly. Thanks to her own big mouth and Jeff's, she was stuck with being a fortune-teller.

"Hey, I've got a whole book of riddles," Ben said. "I could run a riddle booth—my mom would probably bake cakes as prizes in case anybody solves them."

Soon they'd all figured out specialties for themselves. Karen decided not to protest any further. Jeff would probably volunteer her as a tarantula tamer or snake charmer instead.

She dodged outside afterwards so he wouldn't have a chance to pester her.

The late bus wouldn't be along for another half hour, but at least the rain had stopped. Karen paced along a covered walkway to the quad, replaying in her mind all the clever retorts she should have made to Jeff.

"Hey, don't wear a hole in the bricks!" It was

35

Elaine, who looked like a daffodil in her yellow slicker.

"Oh, hi! What are you doing here?" Karen asked.

"I had some work to do on the yearbook," Elaine explained. "What's going on, anyway? It looked as if you and Jeff were having a heavy heart-to-heart this morning, and then you stalked away like he was your worst enemy."

"Oh, Elaine, he's impossible!" Karen burst out. In a rush, she told about the conversation that morning and Jeff's remarks during the Community Service Committee session.

"He's the most impossible boy I ever met!" Karen finished, ignoring the curious stares of a couple of sophomore girls who were also heading for the bus. "I hate him!"

"You'd better be careful," Elaine said as they walked. "Carl says hating somebody is almost the same as loving them."

"That's ridiculous." Karen jammed her hands into her raincoat pockets.

"I know it sounds contradictory," Elaine admitted, "but when you think about it, it makes sense."

"How?" Karen bit her lip. She wasn't exactly in the mood for a lesson in applied psychology.

"Because it means you have strong feelings toward him." Elaine waved one hand for emphasis and then had to grab onto her books to keep from dropping them. "The opposite of love isn't hate, it's indifference."

"That's silly," Karen muttered. She'd hoped Elaine would have something helpful to say.

"Is it?" Elaine pulled a quarter out of the pocket of

her slicker. "See this coin? Imagine heads stands for hate and tails stands for love."

Resignedly, Karen reached for the coin and examined it. "Okay. So what? They're about as far from each other as they can get."

"It does look that way at first, until you realize that they're both on the same coin. You can't separate them. Like you and Jeff. It's funny how you're always together."

"That's just because he likes to poke fun at me. I think when he has to be away from his video games, he needs some other kind of challenge, and unfortunately I'm it," Karen said, groping for excuses, for ways to deny the truth of what Elaine had said. How, after all these years, after all their battles, could she turn around and admit that, yes, what she and Jeff—the boy who'd insulted her more times than there were grains of sand on the beach—felt for each other was love? Impossible! Insane! Yet, if Elaine's theory wasn't true, why did she grow weak in the knees whenever Jeff came near her?

"Maybe." Elaine didn't look convinced. "Hey, would you like to come over to my house Friday night? You could stay over and we'd really have a chance to talk."

"Sure, I'd like that a lot!" Karen gave a little skip as they reached the shelter and joined the younger girls underneath. "You don't have a date with Carl?"

Elaine got a funny look on her face. "No. He likes to have time to himself—to read, I guess. I don't see why we couldn't read and be together, but he says it's not the same thing."

The bus wheezed up, and it wasn't until she got

home that Karen remembered that Friday night was also the night her mother was going out with Mr. Becker.

For a moment, as she scratched Garfield behind the ears, Karen considered staying home. But why? She didn't expect to chase Mr. Becker away, did she? And they'd hardly be likely to take her on their date as a chaperone!

She could just see it. Mom and Mr. Becker would be sitting in the front seat of the car in the drive-in, and Karen would be riding guard in the back, wearing her bathrobe and pink curlers. The thought made her smile.

Every time Anne and Mr. Becker started to kiss, she'd whap them with a rolled-up newspaper.

Karen groaned at the idea.

It was a good thing she was going to Elaine's Friday night, she decided. Otherwise she'd drive herself crazy imagining things that were never going to happen.

Never.

Chapter Four

On Thursday, instead of going directly home from school, Karen took a city bus to the mall.

She felt kind of foolish, going from one store to another asking if they had any information on fortune-telling, but she wasn't sure where to start. The one thing Karen felt sure of was that she *didn't* want to get a Halloween-type costume and make up nonsense fortunes.

At the bookstore, she found a paperback about a type of fortune-telling called the tarot. "What's that?" Karen asked the saleswoman, who was wearing dark-rimmed glasses that were too heavy for her thin face.

"It's a special deck of cards used for telling the future," the woman said. "We don't have them here, but you might check at the gift store."

Karen bought the paperback just in case, then walked to the Glenwood Gift Shop at the other end of the mall.

A few minutes of browsing led her to a shelfful of various deck of cards. One was marked *tarot,* and the picture on the front, of a girl kneeling in front of a lion and holding its jaws open, resembled the one on the cover of her new book.

"That looks like us."

Karen turned sharply, startled by Jeff's voice. He was pointing to the illustration on the cover.

"What do you mean?" she asked, surprised to see him. He seemed to be popping up everywhere these days!

"It sort of reminded me of you, I guess, because you're smaller than me but you always hold your own." Jeff's eyes were sparkling, and the look on his face suddenly made her feel warm.

She noticed that his new blue sweat shirt brought out the color of his eyes. Also, standing so close together, Karen found herself keenly aware of how tall he was — not towering over her, but big enough to shelter her.

Shelter her? She must be going crazy! Jeff probably meant he'd like to feed her to the lions!

"What are you doing here?" she asked.

"Oh, sometimes they carry new video games." He shrugged.

For one split second she thought that maybe he'd followed her there, then she decided she must be hallucinating.

"Let me see that." Jeff took the deck of cards, his hand lightly brushing hers as he did. The touch made her heart flip-flop. "You planning to study up for the carnival?"

"I might as well." Karen led the way to the front counter and paid for the cards. "Who knows, maybe I have hidden talents."

It was the perfect opening for a smart-aleck remark, but he didn't make one. Maybe that was because he didn't have an audience, Karen decided.

"I'm curious about this. Why don't we have something to drink, and we can look them over?" Jeff suggested.

Feeling a bit off-center, Karen agreed, and they went to a little café in the mall. They ordered soft drinks and then spread out the cards across the table.

"It looks like there are four suits, kind of like clubs, spades, hearts, and diamonds, only they're called swords, wands, cups, and pentacles," he said.

Karen flipped through the book. "Plus there's a special group, called the Greater Arcana." She examined some of the extra cards on the table and discovered each had a name, such as Fortitude and Death. "Boy, that's kind of scary. What if you told somebody's fortune and came up with Death?"

"Don't let them see the cards," Jeff advised. "Besides, you'd have to be crazy to really take this stuff seriously."

They read through the book together. There was a lot of information about the history of the cards and how the Gypsies had used them.

But Karen thought the most interesting part was that every card in the deck had a different picture: a king with a sword, a merchant distributing charity to beggars, a young man daydreaming under a tree. Each card had a special meaning, too, and when they were laid upside down, even these meanings changed.

The book also showed them how to lay out the cards. They learned that the position of each card, in relation to the others on the table, meant something different. For example, a card might tell a person something about his future, about his family life, or about the obstacles facing him.

Karen wondered what would happen if after she became proficient she tried to tell her own fortune. She remembered hearing somewhere, though, that psychics could never see their own futures. Well, she sure wasn't going to try with Jeff around!

He pointed to a card that was marked the Six of Cups. The picture on the front showed two children, a boy and and a girl, playing in front of a cottage.

"We used to play like that," Jeff said. "Remember the time I put the fake inkblot on your book report?"

"The joke was on you," Karen recalled with a laugh. "I dumped real ink in your lap before I realized you hadn't actually spoiled my report."

"Yeah. You never took my jokes lying down," he teased.

Karen looked over at him and felt her breath catch in her throat. What were they doing here, having a soda together in the mall as if this were a date or something?

It didn't make sense — she knew this wasn't a date, and yet she actually felt nervous about being with Jeff Becker! He poked his ice cubes around in the bottom of his cup with the straw. "You know, Dad's planning to take her out to dinner."

"Her" obviously referred to Karen's mother. "So?"

"I can't believe the way he's acting," Jeff went on. "He actually bought a bottle of after-shave lotion!"

"That might be going a bit far." Karen tried to keep a straight face. "But have you tried deodorant?"

He shot her a wry look but didn't respond in kind. "Is your mom excited about Friday night? I suppose mothers confide in their daughters about stuff like that."

"She hasn't had time, they've been so busy at the clinic," Karen said. "I guess the cold weather makes animals sick, just like people."

"Maybe it won't be so bad." Jeff hadn't really been listening to her, she realized as he mused on. "One date—I mean, you can go on a couple of dates with somebody before you figure out they've got air in their head."

Was he referring to their week at the beach? Karen wondered with a sudden pang. Probably as soon as she'd gone back to Glenwood, he'd realized he didn't care about her at all.

All of a sudden, she panicked. Look what was happening to her—she was becoming sentimental again and turning into mush! She had to escape quickly before she said something dumb that would give away her true feelings.

"I've got to go fix dinner." She stood up abruptly, nearly snatching the tarot cards out of his hands. "And I don't have much time to study up on this, so I'd better get busy." The fair was a week from next Monday.

"You haven't even told me what you're going to wear yet." Jeff remained sitting, stretching his legs in front of him. "I picture a long paisley skirt and some kind of frilly blouse." He grinned. "Something that'll really set off that red mane of yours."

"I thought I'd borrow one of your ragged T-shirts. We could probably get some extra donations from people who'll feel sorry for me," Karen retorted good-naturedly.

When they were finished, Jeff insisted on accompanying her to the bus. It was jammed, and he held her elbow lightly as they jockeyed for seats. Karen felt as if she were going to melt into a puddle right there on the floor. Darn Jeff! Why did he have to make her feel this way?

"I'm sure everything's going to be all right," Jeff said as they descended at their corner. "Don't worry."

Karen wasn't sure, as she hurried toward her house, whether he was referring to their parents, the fortune-telling, or something else altogether.

Chapter Five

On Friday night, Karen discovered Elaine's house to be, if possible, even more chaotic than hers.

It was a sprawling Victorian full of the oddest assortment of furniture Karen had ever seen. Not that it looked shabby, but she had the feeling Elaine's mother must buy one item at a time, depending on her mood that day, without worrying about what style it was.

The household included a shaggy dog named Buster Brown and a cat named Munchkin, who reminded her a little bit of her beloved Garfield.

And three younger sisters were definitely louder than two older brothers, she decided, especially the seven-year-old twins, Chrissie and Carla, who were fighting over a doll.

Karen was surprised to find she wasn't the only guest. Elaine led her into the den, where Lori Woodhouse was sitting on the Colonial-style sofa with her feet resting on a Danish-modern stool. Lori gave Karen a shy grin.

Lori was one of Elaine's best friends, and one of the most beautiful girls at Glenwood High. She wanted to be a model, and it was easy to see why. With her long, silky blond hair and perfect figure, Karen found it hard to believe Lori had once been fat, before she moved to Glenwood.

In addition to being gorgeous, she also had what the magazines called flair. Right now she was wearing a soft beige-and-blue tweed sleeveless sweater, the kind with giant armholes, over a tan turtleneck and a soft-blue skirt. She looked sensational.

"I hope I'm not in the way," Lori said, even though it was Karen who was the new arrival. "I promised to baby-sit for my neighbor, so I've got to leave in a few minutes anyway."

"I love your outfit." Karen plopped down in an overstuffed chair.

"Gee, thanks." Lori glanced down, as if she'd forgotten what she was wearing. The girls talked for a little while, then Andrea, Elaine's fourteen-year-old sister, came in with a tray of iced tea, and Lori stood up to go. "We'll have to get together another time, Karen."

After she left, Karen and Elaine went upstairs to Elaine's attic bedroom. Andrea followed them into the room and perched on the bed, as if she'd been invited.

The two older girls exchanged muted smiles, silently agreeing to let Andrea stay for a few minutes so her feelings wouldn't be hurt.

Karen glanced around Elaine's bedroom, which

was long and narrow; almost everything in it was some shade of violet. The best feature was the sky-light overhead. You could see the early stars just beginning to come out.

"Do you have a boyfriend?" Andrea asked bluntly as Karen set her overnight case in a corner.

"No," she answered. "Do you?"

Andrea shook her head. "Is your hair naturally that color? I've never seen that shade of red before. It kind of glows." Elaine started laughing, and finally Karen joined in. She knew Andrea meant well.

"Well, when I was a kid," Karen said, glancing at herself in the mirror, "everybody said I looked like Little Orphan Annie."

"Well, if you were, I'll bet Jeff would've wanted to adopt you," Elaine observed, perching on top of her seat.

"Who's Jeff?" Andrea asked.

"This—guy I know," Karen said, feeling herself grow warm at the mere mention of him.

"Not Jeff Becker?" Andrea's eyes turned into big O's. "Boy, he's really cute. I see him on the bus all the time. Does he have a girl friend?"

"Not that I know of," Karen said, remembering how she'd seen him climb into a car with cheer-leader Marcia Connors after school that afternoon. Suddenly, she felt alarmed.

Elaine apparently decided that enough was enough. "Andrea, Karen and I have a few things we want to talk about privately."

"Oh. Okay." The younger girl shrugged and ambled out reluctantly. She turned, lingering in the doorway. "Is it hard finding makeup with your complexion, Karen? Did you used to have freckles? How did you get rid of them?"

" 'Bye, Andrea." Elaine advanced toward her sister, who scooted down the stairs. As soon as Andrea was out of sight, she sighed and rolled her eyes. "My sister, the household pest!"

"We probably were, too, at that age," Karen said, "although Fred and Zack were always very patient with me. In fact, I think Zack's much more impatient now than he used to be. These days, he always seems to be running around somewhere or on the telephone."

"Yes, I know." Elaine got a dreamy look in her eyes. She'd taken out her contact lenses and was wearing her old tortoiseshell glasses, but she had such large, dark eyes that you could still see them clearly.

"You do?" Karen groaned. "Oh, no. Are you mad at me for giving him your phone number? I figured you could always say no."

"Mad?" Elaine looked surprised. "No, I'm glad you did. He called me up on Tuesday, and we talked for an hour, until my mother made me get off the phone, and then we did the same thing again on Wednesday"—she hesitated before adding—"and Thursday."

Karen couldn't believe it. Elaine talking for hours on the phone, with Zack? Elaine couldn't possibly have a crush on him, could she? Not that he wasn't sort of cute, but, well, he wore mismatched laces on his tennis shoes, and when he caught cold his nose turned all red like Bozo the Clown's. "What on earth did you talk about?"

"Everything," Elaine said, hugging a stuffed alligator. "I didn't realize it was possible to feel so comfortable just rapping with a guy."

" 'Everything,' like what?" Karen persisted.

"Well—like what college is like. Oh, I almost forgot!" Elaine reached under the bed and pulled out a box of doughnuts. "I hid them here so the twins wouldn't find them. Want one?"

Karen couldn't resist. She picked out a glazed doughnut with chocolate melted on top. "Wouldn't Carl mind if he found out?"

Elaine lost her dreamy look. "That's the problem." She sighed. "I really care about Carl. I've always been able to talk things over with him, too, but my conversations with Zack are so different. More— electric, somehow. Do you know what I mean?"

Karen thought about the way she'd felt when Jeff's hand brushed hers at the gift shop and shivered. "So what are you going to do?" she said quickly.

"I don't know. Got any bright ideas?" Munchkin joined Elaine on the bed, and she ran her hand across the cat's furry back. A soft, rumbling purr filled the room.

Karen remembered the tarot cards and pulled them from her overnight case.

"Look at these." She explained them to Elaine. "I've been studying them like crazy—I stayed up till two o'clock last night, and I took the book to school today so I could study every spare minute. They're really wild—there're seventy-eight of them, and every one has at least a couple of meanings."

"Wow!" Elaine knelt on the rug with her, studying the colorful pictures. "What did you find out about your future?"

Karen helped herself to an orange-covered dough-nut. After all, she needed the mental energy to con-centrate on the cards. "Well," she hedged, "they say you can't tell your own fortune, and I think it's true. The cards haven't made sense when I've tried. Maybe that's for the best, though."

"Then tell my fortune!" Elaine said, shuffling the cards back together into a heap.

"Sure." Karen flipped through the deck and pulled out a card. It was the Queen of Pentacles, which showed a pretty woman sitting on a throne. The woman possessed a certain calm self-awareness that reminded Karen of Elaine.

"This will be your indicator," Karen explained. "It sits in the middle, and I lay the other cards around it. But you have to promise not to take anything I say too seriously, Elaine. Especially since I'm just a beginner."

"Okay, I promise." But Elaine clutched her hands together eagerly as Karen spread the cards on the bed.

"You have to ask me a yes-or-no question to help me understand what the cards are saying," Karen continued as she finished laying out the cards. "And it has to be about something that's going on right now in your life—something like, 'Am I going to get into my first-choice college?' "

"Okay," Elaine said. "My question is, What's going to happen between Carl and me? Were we really meant for each other?"

"That isn't a yes-or-no question." Karen laughed. But she turned her attention to the cards anyway and concentrated.

She felt a little funny, reading the cards for Elaine. It was almost as if she were trespassing on Gypsy territory—getting involved in something she shouldn't. Would some old crone show up on her doorstep and put a hex on her? The stars overhead suddenly looked eerie and far away, not romantic at all. A chill rippled across Karen's arm, raising goose flesh.

"Okay." Karen jumped as Elaine's cheerful voice broke the spell. "Should I tell Carl I've been having these long conversations with Zack?"

"Do you think you need to?" Karen asked, forgetting that Elaine had meant the question for the tarot cards. "I mean, Zack's interesting, but you're not going out with him or anything."

"Well—no," Elaine admitted. "Only I can't understand why I should like another guy so much if I'm in love with Carl."

Karen focused on the cards. After a while she said, "This is funny."

As usual, the cards were anything but clear. For instance, under obstacles Karen had dealt the Seven of Swords, which showed a man—maybe a thief—creeping away from a camp with a bunch of swords. It had several different meanings: it could mean that Elaine was attempting something new, or it could mean that she was involved in a quarrel. Puzzling.

The Six of Cups showed up as the outcome, the most important position. That was the same card Jeff had noticed, the one with the two children playing in front of a cottage. But it was upside down.

"This card—I'm trying to figure out what it

means," Karen admitted. "I have this intuition, but the meaning isn't exactly the same as what the book says. It's supposed to mean that something is about to be renewed, but I've got a feeling that isn't quite right this time."

"Hmmm," Elaine said, her expression noncommittal, "tell me what you think it means!"

"I think the cards are talking about you, and not about Carl or Zack," Karen ventured. "They're saying that you're growing up, putting your childhood behind you, and that the process isn't always easy. I guess having to decide what to do about Carl is part of it."

"Gee." Elaine stared down at the cards thoughtfully. "That's true. Sometimes I think about how much I've grown up in the last few years. Then something else happens, and I have to grow up even more. I wonder how old you have to be before you really feel like an adult."

"Do you sometimes wish you could go back?" Karen asked. She decided she'd said enough and started to gather up the cards carefully and mix them back into the deck.

"Once in a while," Elaine said after a pause. "Especially when I think about next year and how we'll all be scattered across the country doing different things. Of course I'll still see my friends during holidays, but they're always so short, and it won't be the same."

Karen thought about Jeff and how they spent a lot of time together, even though they mostly spent it arguing. Would she miss Jeff? Somehow, the idea of not having him in her life left a strange empty feeling inside her.

"Maybe if I had a boyfriend, I'd want to stay a senior forever," Karen said, "but I don't."

They went to bed in a thoughtful mood, and it wasn't until just before she fell asleep that Karen remembered to worry about her mother's date that night with Mr. Becker.

Chapter Six

Anne Waverly picked Karen up at noon the next day.

The moment she saw her mother's radiant face, Karen felt her pancake breakfast clot into a hard lump in her stomach.

"Did you have a good time last night?" her mother asked.

"Yes," Karen said. "Did you?"

The car backfired as Anne steered it out onto Glenwood's main street and they rattled between rows of picturesque shops now filled with tourists.

"We had dinner at the Fisherman's Catch," her mother said. "I don't think you've ever been there, have you? It's on a cliff overlooking the ocean. We could hear the waves crashing against the shore. The fish was delicious—it tasted as if they'd just caught it."

Karen stared at her mother in alarm. Anne was

usually plainspoken and to-the-point. Now she sounded as if she wanted to burst into song.

"Did you go to a movie or something afterwards?" she asked.

"Believe it or not, we just sat in the car and talked for a couple of hours," Anne said.

Sat in the car? Karen's throat tightened. Was it possible her mother had actually kissed Mr. Becker?

"Karen, you're awfully quiet," her mother said. "Is something wrong?"

"No, of course not." Her voice came out in a little squeak.

Pulling into their driveway, Anne turned to Karen. "I know this must be unsettling for you. I haven't dated anyone seriously since your father died. But you know I'd never do anything that would hurt you or the boys."

The only thing that registered with Karen was the word *seriously*. Her mother must have strong feelings about Mr. Becker to talk that way!

"You know I want you to be happy, Mom," Karen managed to say. That certainly was true.

Her mother gave her a quick hug. "I'm just dropping you off. I promised Art I'd take over at the clinic this afternoon."

Karen wandered into the house, feeling lost. She looked around as she had the other day, seeing the worn, familiar furniture with new eyes—this time wondering what it would be like if Jeff and his father lived there.

Maybe they'd even move into a bigger house, but what difference would it make? She'd still have to face Jeff at breakfast and at dinner every day.

He'd see her in her curlers and bathrobe, and he'd be hanging around when her friends came over to visit.

Even more awful, he'd be around when she had a date. And she'd have to watch him getting ready to go out on dates, too.

Did he date much? Karen wondered as she went up to her bedroom and unpacked her nightgown. He usually did bring someone when he went to weekend parties. But then again, she often had a date, too. Had he taken Sherri Cunningham out recently? Or somebody else, like beautiful, popular Marcia Connors who gave him a ride to who-knows-where on Friday afternoon?

She felt a dart of jealousy at the thought, which made her angry. Why should she care who Jeff went out with?

She studied her room, wondering what he'd think of it. The furniture was white French provincial, which her mother had picked out when Karen was a little girl. She especially liked the bed, which had a pink canopy, even though it was a pain to wash and iron.

As usual, Anne had left receipts and canceled checks in separate envelopes on Karen's desk. Now she pulled out the brown ledger book and began neatly penciling the amounts into the proper columns.

The precision of the task steadied her. She wished life were like accounting: you put the figures in the proper columns, and they added up neatly and predictably. No surprises. No potato bugs in your lunch box.

As she was double-checking her work, she heard some rustling noises in Fred's room across the hall. Impulsively Karen walked over and knocked.

"Come in." He sounded a bit tired, even though it was barely past noon.

Karen opened the door and stepped inside. The walls of her brother's room, which used to be covered with posters of Bruce Springsteen and surfers, now sported medical illustrations of various parts of the anatomy. She wondered if they gave Fred nightmares. The floor was covered with books, and the air smelled musty. Instinctively, Karen walked over to the window and opened it.

Fred looked up from his desk, where he'd been reading and taking notes by the light of a small lamp. His eyes were red.

It was funny how, trying to look at him objectively, she could see the resemblance to Zack. Fred's hair was almost the same shade of brown, although better tamed, and his eyes were only a slightly paler blue.

And yet her older brother looked entirely different. He had a rangier frame and more prominent cheekbones — kind of like Clint Eastwood, Karen decided.

"Don't you ever take a break?" she scolded.

"Getting into medical school is really competitive these days," he said, but he gave her a welcoming grin. "Have a seat, if you can find a spot that isn't full of books."

Karen sat on a straight wooden chair. "I wanted to ask your opinion about Mom."

"What about Mom?"

"About her dating."

57

"You mean Albert Becker?" Fred stretched his legs out and laced his hands behind his head. "Albert's a nice guy, I guess. Kind of quiet, but that's all right."

It sounded funny to hear Fred call Mr. Becker by his first name. Suddenly it struck Karen that her brother was nearly a grown-up, that he'd begun to identify more with their mother than with being a teenager. In fact, he'd be twenty in a few months.

She decided to come right to the point. "What bothers me is Mr. Becker's son, Jeff. He drives me crazy. I couldn't live in the same house with him."

"Oh? You planning to move in with him?" Fred lifted an eyebrow, Groucho style.

"Not on your life!" She stared at him in horror.

"Then I guess there's nothing to worry about." Absentmindedly, Fred rubbed the bridge of his nose. Karen remembered that their father used to do that, too, when he'd been reading.

"Unless Mom decides to get married," Karen pointed out. "You don't think she would do that, though, do you? I mean we've been happy all this time, right? She earns a good living, and she's so busy she hardly has time to breathe."

"Yeah." Fred was watching her closely, and Karen stared back at him. "I'll bet she's really looking forward to the next few years, when we go off to college and get married and so on and she'll be rattling around this big house by herself. Or were you planning on staying right here?"

"Well, not forever," Karen had to admit. "Honestly, I don't mind if she gets married again. I just don't want Jeff Becker for a stepbrother."

"If Mom comes in humming 'The Hawaiian Wedding Song' and weaving baby's breath through her hair, you let me know and I'll start worrying," Fred replied and turned back to his book.

A big help he was! She should have realized that brothers as a species were incapable of sympathy. Karen sighed as she went to clean the bathroom, one of her weekly household chores. Still, Fred's practical words cheered her up, and she resolved not to worry anymore. The resolve lasted for exactly four hours and thirty-seven minutes. That's when Anne disappeared out the door, calling to Karen that she had a dinner date with Mr. Becker!

After sending out for a pizza and devouring it, Karen and Fred went with Zack to a screening at the college. It was a foreign film called *Diva* that started out kind of slow, about a young guy's crush on an opera singer. Then suddenly he got caught up in the middle of a suspense plot, and the rest of the movie whizzed by.

Afterwards, some of Zack's friends came over to talk with them, including a couple of girls who practically hung onto his arms. They all went to the campus snack bar, and over a banana split Karen listened to the others talk about classes and movies and how they were all going to find fame and fortune before they were thirty.

She felt unusually happy, riding home with her brothers in the chugging jalopy. A lot of Saturday nights she had a date, but she rarely had as good a time with any of the boys at school as she'd had tonight. With Zack and Fred she could really be herself. Besides, how many girls had two handsome guys escorting them around?

Anne didn't get home until midnight. Karen pretended to be asleep, but she couldn't help overhearing her mother humming as she got ready for bed in the next room.

On Monday, Jeff Becker caught up with her as they were leaving civics class.

"Hey, don't run off," he said. "I need to talk to you."

Karen swallowed hard. Jeff's expression was earnest. At that moment he looked both sweet and vulnerable. His blond hair was tousled and unkempt, as if he'd rushed out of phys ed—which she knew he had fifth period that afternoon—without combing it. His face was flushed, and the collar of his rugby shirt was open at a strange angle, revealing a section of his tanned throat and chest. In spite of herself, Karen's heart started to pound.

"What about?" She stopped on the sidewalk, moving aside to let some other students pass.

"Our parents," Jeff said, now looking genuinely troubled. "They came over to our house after dinner Saturday and sat out on the porch talking and giggling like a couple of kids. It was embarrassing."

"Wasn't your dad having a good time?" Karen asked.

"Well, sure, I guess so."

"Then what's the problem?" It was funny how she instinctively defended her mother. It was one thing for Karen to have doubts about Anne's romance, but she wouldn't tolerate criticism from anybody else.

"That's not the point. My parents used to have a good time, too, when my sister and I were little"—Jeff leaned against the wall, holding his books in front of him—"but, boy, did things change. They started screaming at each other all the time...I remember lying in bed at night crying, listening to them fight."

"My mom's not like that!" Karen flared. "She's the most reasonable person I ever met!"

"So's my father, and I can't believe he's acting like a—a teenager!" Jeff said. "I'm beginning to think your mother's cast a spell over him."

Karen was annoyed—this time his teasing had cut a little too close to home. "Maybe it's the other way around," she suggested, narrowing her eyes slightly. Jeff looked surprised, then his expression softened. "Touché. I can never get the better of you, can I?"

"Not on your best day." Karen shot him a triumphant grin over her shoulder as she turned to leave.

"Hey, wait a minute." Jeff caught hold of her arm, and his touch set off a funny reaction, a warm tickle that ran up to her shoulder. "We've been friends for a long time, right?"

"Oh, sure," Karen said. "Our antagonism has weathered every storm." But she paused, and his hand lingered on her elbow.

"Maybe we could get together somewhere after school," Jeff suggested.

"I've got a lot of stuff to do." She was torn between wanting to pull away and wanting to stand there forever feeling his hand against her arm.

"Look, I think it's important we discuss this," Jeff persisted. "Otherwise we're likely to find ourselves sharing the toothpaste in the morning and squabbling over who has to take out the garbage."

"I guess you're right," Karen grumbled. "Okay, where do you want to meet?"

They decided on a small park down the street from their houses, where they used to play as children, and finally he let go of Karen's arm.

She could feel him watching her as she walked away. Her hem must be coming loose, she decided, but when she checked it a moment later, it wasn't.

For some strange reason, Karen began to feel excited.

Chapter Seven

She stopped by her house first to drop off her books after school.

No sooner had Karen opened the front door than a series of thumps, squeaks, and meows greeted her. A large crash sent her scurrying into the living room to see what on earth was going on.

Tweety's cage was lying on the floor, with the small yellow bird hopping around inside chirping like crazy while Garfield poked his orange paws through the bars.

"Garfield!" Karen said. "What are you doing?" She looked around for Doggone, who usually kept the cat from sneaking inside.

That's when she realized that not all the squeaking was coming from the living room. Something was chattering a wordless protest at the top of its lungs in the den.

Grabbing Garfield—who meowed plaintively, as if

to ask what he'd done wrong—Karen hurried into the den. But Doggone's ferocious bark, aimed at Garfield, stopped her in the doorway.

The big, ramshackle dog sat in front of the sofa, guarding an open box. Nestled inside was something small and furry and upset.

"What the heck is going on here?" Even as Karen spoke, she realized that Doggone must be protecting whatever was in the box from Garfield. Their fight apparently had carried into the living room, overturning Tweety's cage.

Doggone stalked forward, growling at Garfield. Digging his claws painfully into Karen's arm, the cat tried to climb up her shoulder.

"Ouch!" She dashed through the living room and dumped the cat out the front door, then righted Tweety's cage and hurried back to see what Doggone had been guarding.

A tiny squirrel, its leg in a miniature cast, lay in the box, squeaking pitifully.

"Poor little thing." Karen picked the squirrel up and cradled it in her hands. "Why did Mom leave you on the floor? You must be scared to death."

She held the little animal until its racing heartbeat slowed, then took it to the kitchen and fed it a bit of fresh lettuce. The squirrel was probably one of a family that lived in the Monterey pine in the back yard, she reflected. Smart squirrel, to pick a veterinarian's backyard to get hurt in.

It was just like her mother to help the little creature, but it wasn't like Anne to forget to put an injured wild animal in a safe place. Unless... Karen felt exasperated again as she realized the answer.

Could Anne really be that much in love?

It wasn't until Karen had tucked the squirrel back in its box and carried it to her room, where it would be safe from any and all visitors, that she remembered Jeff was waiting for her at the park.

"Oh!" She raced down the steps and out of the house, nearly stepping on Garfield in her hurry. The cat sputtered in protest at the indignities he had suffered that day, and Karen silently vowed to save part of a hamburger from dinner as a peace offering.

The park was two blocks away, and she was breathless by the time she arrived.

Jeff was waiting in the playground area, an assortment of jungle bars and swings.

Sitting on a bench with his hands thrust deep into the pockets of his Windbreaker, he looked pensive and appealing. There was something about his forlorn expression that tugged at her heart.

Then he spotted her, and his face lit up. "Hey!" He stood and started toward her. "I'd nearly given up hope."

"We had a crisis at the zoo," Karen told him. "Take one dog, one cat, one squirrel, and one parakeet, and mix well."

He touched her arm, just at the spot where Garfield had clawed her, and Karen winced.

"Are you all right?" Jeff's voice deepened with concern.

"Just a few scratches."

"Maybe you should put something on it," he said, but she shook her head.

Karen glanced around. It felt funny to be here, alone with Jeff, as if they were having some kind of romantic rendezvous.

Not that the place was particularly beautiful—a few trees, the playground, and a stretch of grass. And there was a clump of azalea bushes in bloom, an airy froth of white and pink. "Remember how we used to play here when we were kids?"

"Yes. Boy, that seems like centuries ago." Jeff guided her back to the bench. "Are you cold? I suppose we could go somewhere else."

"No, I'm fine." Karen sank down, grateful for the rest. She took a deep breath of the cool, scented air and looked over at her seatmate.

He was studying her with a peculiar expression. His eyes sparkled eagerly, and his lips were slightly parted. For some reason it reminded her of the way Zack had looked at Elaine when they'd started talking about films.

Finally Jeff licked his lips, blinked, and presto chango, there he was, the Jeff she knew all too well, wearing a cocky grin.

"I thought that, well, being Glenwood's resident fortune-teller, maybe you could help me figure out how to break up our parents," he began.

Karen chafed her hands together, feeling annoyed. "My mom doesn't interfere in my life. Why should I mess with hers?"

"You'd be doing her a favor." Jeff reached over and took her hands, rubbing them between his gloved ones. "They'll break up sooner or later. The sooner it is, the less it'll hurt."

Some guys, she thought, when they hold your hand, feel like limp fish. Other guys figure they've suddenly turned into Chuck Norris and do a lot of heavy squeezing. Jeff wasn't like that. He held Karen's hand lightly, but firmly. The contact made Karen feel warm and yielding, yet embarrassed at the same time. After all, Jeff probably didn't mean anything by it. He was just trying to keep her warm.

"Look, I'm not crazy about this big romance either," Karen admitted, "but I don't like acting sneaky. Why don't we tell them flat out how we feel?"

Jeff groaned. "It wouldn't work. Oh, sure, they might take a break from their dating to please us, but absence makes the heart grow fonder, right? Sooner or later they'd get back together, and there'd be wedding bells for sure."

"I've never been a bridesmaid," Karen teased. "Maybe they could get married at the clinic. That way our pets could be there, too. Don't you think Bluto would look nice in a tux?"

Jeff couldn't resist. "I've heard of ceremonies where they turn doves loose at the end. How about your parakeet? It could sort of flap around the room and chirp."

"And drop lime on everybody?" Karen made a face. "We'd have to warn the guests to bring umbrellas."

"What a great wedding — dogs underfoot and birds in your hair." Jeff chuckled, and then suddenly his smile vanished. "What am I laughing about?"

"About our parents getting married." The sun was starting to set, and a cool breeze made her shiver. Almost without thinking, she moved closer to Jeff, to get warm.

He had stopped rubbing her hands but still held them. "No, I'm serious, Karen. It won't work. They'd be happy for a little while, and then they'd make each other miserable."

"My parents were happy together," she pointed out. "Why don't you think it would work?"

"Because I know my dad." Jeff gazed off into the distance. "He's really sensitive. I'm the only one who knows how to cheer him up when he gets down and humor him along when he gets grouchy."

"Like I get coffee for my mom?" It was strange to think of Jeff doing the same kinds of things for his father.

"Well, for instance, on Sundays, I know he enjoys this kind of ritual we have. We get up early and go out for doughnuts. Then we buy the Sunday paper on the way home and read the comics to each other."

"You do?" Karen grinned, imagining the scene. Jeff would have on a torn T-shirt and one of those baseball caps he liked to wear backwards. His father, most likely, would drive, while Jeff, slouched back in his seat, would read animatedly, pausing for just a split second before the punch line.

Abruptly, Jeff leaned back on the bench, letting go of her hands, which felt cold all over again. "You know what else? On Saturdays, sometimes Dad and I watch the cartoons on TV."

"You do?" Karen turned toward him, curling one leg up on the seat to get more comfortable. "Sometimes Mom and I watch tapes of *The Muppet Show*," she admitted with a giggle.

"They're great," Jeff agreed. "But with Dad—I don't think it's really the cartoons he likes. It's the ritual. Doing the same thing every week, knowing he can count on it—and on me."

68

"But Mom said he wanted to take a photo safari to Africa," Karen pointed out.

"Oh, sure, he talks about it, but the truth is, when something unpredictable happens, like problems at work, he gets furious." Jeff scuffed at the sidewalk with one tennis shoe. "Sometimes he stays that way for days. Mom said he was moody, and she couldn't take it anymore."

"So?" Karen watched the last rays of the sun play across Jeff's face, catching a glint of sadness in his eyes. "That doesn't mean my mother..."

"Trust me. I know what I'm talking about." Jeff fiddled with the zipper of his jacket. "They'll hurt each other really bad, the way my parents did."

What if Mom fell deeply in love with Mr. Becker and then everything came apart? Karen thought. She'd be heartbroken. Mr. Becker did sound moody and hard to live with. Probably he could be charming on a date; even Jeff was nice once in a while. Then after they got married, he'd turn out to be like Dr. Jekyll and Mr. Hyde. Mom had no idea what she was letting herself in for.

Karen thought about one Saturday a few weeks ago when she and her mother had sat together in the kitchen over a pitcher of lemonade. Anne had talked about her first day at college, how she'd gotten lost and embarrassed herself by bursting into tears. Karen had felt really close to her then, closer than ever before.

The opportunities for that kind of sharing, that kind of intimacy would be gone, if her mother and Mr. Becker got married. Especially if they fought all the time. And Jeff knew his father best. If he said his

69

dad was hard to live with, he was probably right.

"If we're not going to tell them how we feel, how do you think we should try to break them up?" Absentmindedly, she toyed with a sprig of pink flowers on an azalea bush next to the bench. "I mean, if I decided we ought to."

"I was hoping you might think of something," Jeff admitted. "You're always full of clever ideas."

"Me?" A couple of blossoms came off in, Karen's hand.

Jeff leaned toward her eagerly. "Hey, what if we planted clues to make it look as if Dad were dating around? Wouldn't your mom get mad and stop seeing him?"

"But if he's taking her out on Friday and Saturday nights, when is he supposed to be dating other women?" Karen pointed out.

"Yeah, I suppose it's not a very good idea." Jeff traced his thumb along Karen's shoulder, leaving a trail of warmth that caused her to break out in goose bumps. "Your mom would probably get jealous and possessive and really sink her hooks into him."

"My mother's not like that!" Karen jerked away from him and dropped the flowers. "She's beautiful and smart and independent. Don't you talk about her that way!"

"I'm sorry." Jeff ducked his head ruefully. "I don't know why I said that. I didn't mean it."

"You have strange ideas about women." Karen stood up and began pacing. It was too cold to keep sitting. "Maybe that's what comes from growing up with only men in the house."

Jeff walked alongside her. "Maybe so. I never could

understand girls."

"You think boys are easy to figure out?" She shook her head. There was nothing complicated about girls, not as far as she could see. But guys! They could drive you crazy.

They walked together under a row of pine trees. The needles gave off a crisp, tangy scent that reminded Karen of a campground in the mountains where she'd stayed with her family a few years ago.

Finally, Jeff broke the silence. "How about if you pretend to have a fatal illness? Your mom would be so wrapped up taking care of you that she wouldn't have time to date."

For a moment, Karen wasn't sure whether or not he was kidding. "Oh, that's a great idea, Jeff. And just how do you pretend to have a fatal illness?"

"I don't know." Jeff shrugged. "In the movies, people have dizzy spells and faint a lot."

"In real life, you go to a doctor and they stick needles in you and do X rays and don't let you go to school," Karen pointed out, scuffing at a pinecone. "That's a dumb idea."

"Okay, it's a dumb idea," he agreed, smiling.

"On the other hand," Karen said, "if we stay out here much longer, we might both freeze to death, which would solve the problem."

"I know how to warm us up! I'll bet I can swing higher than you can." Jeff caught her hand and began to run, catching her off-balance.

Pulled along, Karen stumbled against him, feeling the solid support of his shoulder as he steadied her.

"Hey, careful," he said.

In the cold air, their breath made clouds that just

touched each other. Karen's heart beat wildly. It was almost like kissing.

She pulled away and dashed ahead of him. "You can't either swing higher than me! I was the champion, remember?"

"Yeah, but that was a long time ago!" He tested one of the swings to make sure it was strong enough, then pushed off from the ground. "Besides, you're a girl!"

"Anything you can do, I can do better!" Karen sang out, swinging into motion.

They rocked back and forth, thrusting themselves higher and higher above the ground. The breeze felt cold but exhilarating against her face, and Karen laughed with unexpected delight. She'd forgotten what the world looked like from the top of a swing.

They both continued pumping madly, bringing their legs back and then kicking forward. It was a contest, and Karen was winning. Then suddenly, Jeff began to gain on her.

Karen's mop of red curls flew around her face. She could hardly see, and yet she couldn't stop laughing. "No! No, you're not going to catch up with me!"

"Oh, yes I am!" Jeff called out. And in the next instant as Karen stretched out her legs to break her forward momentum, he pulled up and fell in sync with her long, rhythmic swings. They were even.

"Hey, maybe we'd better knock it off," Jeff called. "I think we're getting carried away."

"Speak for yourself!" she answered.

A minute later, he jumped down. The sudden motion jarred the swing set and sent Karen heading kitty-corner toward a pole.

She twisted in her seat and leaped off blindly, falling smack into Jeff.

They tumbled down in a tangle of arms and legs, hitting the worn grass with a thud.

Lying there half on top of Jeff sent a shock wave of new feelings racing through Karen. And she could see from the way his eyes widened and his arms tightened around her that he felt the same way.

For one scary, thrilling moment, she thought he was going to kiss her.

Then he untangled himself and pulled her to her feet. "I guess you're not cold anymore, huh?" he teased.

Karen was trembling, but not from the cold. She lowered her face so he wouldn't see she was blushing. "No. Look," she said, her voice sounding distant and unnatural, "I've got to go fix dinner."

"Let's sit on the wheel. Just for a minute." He pulled her across the hard, bare ground of the playground. "We haven't figured out what we're going to do yet."

They sat on the wheel, still breathing fast, and Jeff began gently moving them in a circle.

"I used to dream about being an astronaut," Jeff admitted. "But after that workout on the swings, I don't think I've got the stamina for it. I'll tell you, if we could bring our parents out here and let them work up a sweat, they wouldn't have the energy to carry on a romance."

"Does your dad like to exercise?" Karen asked.

"No, but he should," Jeff said. "I'm always telling him to join a health club or start jogging or something. My grandfather died of a heart attack when he was about fifty, and I'm afraid of something like that happening to Dad."

They looked at each other, both of them getting the idea at the same time.

"You know, if . . ." Jeff started.

"I could . . ." Karen said, and they both halted. "You go first."

He nodded. "Maybe I could get my father exercising and wear him out. Lots of cold showers—that's what he needs to get his circulation going and his libido down."

"What's libido?" Karen asked and then blushed furiously. "Don't worry, it's not what you think," Jeff assured her, smiling. "It means—desire, I guess."

Karen spoke up quickly to hide her embarrassment. "Mom doesn't have time to exercise, she's busy at the clinic."

"Is there any way you could get her any busier?" Jeff said.

"I'm not going to start a rabies epidemic, that's for sure!" Karen leaned back against his shoulder. She could feel his muscles move rhythmically as he rotated the wheel.

Jeff took a moment to answer, and then his voice sounded husky. "Well . . . um . . . how about if you said you were having trouble in school and asked her to help with your homework?"

"On Saturday night?" Karen gazed out at the park, noticing how the rosebushes were already budding. "Still, you've got a point. I could pretend to be having some problems in French. Parents always get upset if they think their kids are having trouble."

"You could feel an attack of F's coming on every

time she gets near the telephone or starts to go out in the evening," Jeff prompted.

Karen sighed. She didn't like being dishonest with her mother, but this would be for Anne's own good. "I'll do my best."

"We'll call it Operation Split," Jeff declared. "That way, if we mention it when other people are around, they won't know what we're talking about."

He walked Karen home, taking her hand in his on the pretense that he wanted to keep her fingers warm. They paused in front of her house, talking in the semidarkness, and for a moment, Karen thought he was going to pull her into his arms. But he didn't.

Well, who wanted him to, anyway? she told herself as she twisted away and stomped inside.

The warmth of the house came as a relief after the unusually cold evening air, but she missed having her hand in Jeff's. Wistfully, she pulled off her jacket and went up to check on the squirrel.

Chapter Eight

Fortunately, that night Karen had planned an easy dinner—hamburgers with potato chips—since she didn't have much time to get it ready.

Fred was upstairs studying, so Zack set the table and poured four glasses of ice water.

"Where have you been?" he asked.

It wasn't like Zack to be nosy. Most of the time he hardly noticed whether she was home or not.

"I got together with a friend," Karen said, kneading dry onion soup mix into the ground meat before forming patties.

"Elaine?" he asked as he unscrewed the saltshaker and refilled it. It seemed to Karen that he was moving at a snail's pace, perhaps to prolong the conversation.

"No, somebody else," Karen said, remaining evasive. She molded the patties carefully. "Elaine told me you two have been talking a lot on the phone."

76

"She's really fun to talk to." Zack leaned against the counter. "When I was in high school, it seemed like the girls in my class were only interested in clothes and makeup. Elaine's not like that—she's got a healthy intellectual curiosity about everything."

"Elaine's probably the smartest kid in the senior class, except for Carl," Karen replied. She couldn't resist adding, "Carl's her boyfriend, you know."

"I know." Zack sounded troubled. "But it's funny. She says they're going together and all, but the way she talks about him, he sounds more like a good friend than someone she's really in love with."

Karen, kneeling at the broiler, observed, "I think it's nice that they're such good friends. Being head over heels in love makes people act dopey." She was thinking of her mom.

"Maybe that's what Elaine is looking for," Zack replied mysteriously, "a little more romance in her life."

While Karen was still trying to decide what he meant by that, their mother arrived home. As soon as she came into the kitchen, Karen told her about the fight between Doggone and Garfield.

"Oh, no!" Anne burst out. "I finished setting the squirrel's leg, and then Albert called, and I forgot all about him! Where is he?"

A few minutes later, she came down from Karen's bedroom holding the box. "He looks none the worse for wear," Anne announced. She chattered on about how she'd found him, but Karen scarcely heard a word. She was too busy feeling guilty about the plans to disrupt her mother's romance.

On the other hand, did Anne really need a man

like Mr. Becker?

Anybody could see her mom was beautiful. The first thing you noticed was the thick auburn hair, and then her graceful way of moving. Even though she usually stuck to slacks and blouses, they looked great on her. She could probably get any man she wanted. In fact, Karen wished she had more of her mom's style and flair. She thought about Elaine and Lori and how sharp they looked. Maybe they could give her some advice.

Anne left the kitchen and then trekked back with a cage from the garage. Her hair was floating around in wisps as if she'd been digging through piles of junk, as she probably had; the garage was so full of stuff they couldn't park the cars in it. "Boy, things have been going crazy at the clinic—I guess it's the weather. I'm beginning to feel like I need a vacation."

It was as good a cue as any, Karen figured. Taking a deep breath, she plunged in. "That's a good idea! You hardly ever take time off, Mom. Why don't you go somewhere for a few days, like maybe Hawaii?"

Her mother laughed. "Thanks. I hope you've been saving up your allowance, because I certainly can't afford it."

Karen sighed and took the hamburger buns out of the oven. This wasn't going to be easy.

They were just finishing dinner when her mother said casually, "I hope you kids don't mind cleaning up. I've got a date."

"With Mr. Becker?" Karen asked, and Anne nodded. She'd better think quickly! "Um—I was hoping you could help me with my French. I'm having a hard time, and you speak it so well."

78

"You've never had trouble with your classes before." Anne frowned as she cleared the dishes and brought out a carton of ice cream.

"I—I guess I'm having a hard time concentrating," Karen improvised. "I don't know why. The last week or so, I've been kind of distracted. We've got a test tomorrow, and I'm afraid I'll flunk."

"Well, we can't have that," Anne said. "Albert won't mind . . ."

"I'll coach her." Fred helped himself to a dollop of ice cream.

Karen wanted to kick him under the table. "But you've got your own studying," she said sweetly, gritting her teeth. "If you want to transfer to get into medical school . . ."

"A couple of hours won't make any difference." Fred shot her a knowing look, and Karen got the message. He'd figured it out! There was nothing left to say, she reflected glumly. She could hardly admit the truth to her mother.

As soon as Anne left for her date, Fred carried an armload of Karen's French books downstairs.

She stood with her hands on her hips, glaring at him. "I don't really need this."

"Why, of course you do," he said innocently, spreading everything out on the kitchen table. "What would Mom think if she came home and I told her you refused to study?"

Karen plopped onto one of the chairs. This was blackmail, but what could she do about it? Obviously Fred planned to teach her a lesson—one that had nothing to do with French. "Okay, prof, go ahead," she grumbled.

"The verb *aimer* — to love — conjugate it," he said.

As soon as she finished, he said, "Now how about *se marier*, to get married." He managed to keep a straight face.

"Oh, give me a break!" Karen groaned.

He closed the book with an exaggerated sigh. "Well, okay, but Mom's sure going to be disappointed."

Karen smacked her hand down on the table and said, glaring at her brother, *"Se marier. Je me marie, tu..."*

Fred wasn't satisfied until she'd spent a full hour conjugating verbs. It didn't make her feel any better, either, when Anne came home so merry she danced Doggone around the den.

Jeff took the seat beside Karen on the bus the next morning. "I guess we didn't do too well last night," he said glumly.

"I did my best," Karen retorted. "I told her I needed tutoring. I ended up spending a whole hour studying French with my brother Fred, which is not my idea of a good time, and then I had to spend the rest of the evening working on the tarot cards."

"I think we need a new game plan for Operation Split," Jeff said. "Why don't we meet this afternoon at Gennaro's?"

"We've got Social Service Committee, remember?" Karen pointed out.

"Oh, right. Well, the meeting shouldn't last long. We can walk over to the pizza place afterwards."

"Okay," Karen acquiesced. She didn't see how she could get out of it gracefully. Besides, they were in this together, weren't they?

80

The rain that had dampened Glenwood for the past week began drizzling again during the morning, and the students had to eat in the cafeteria instead of sitting outside as they usually did.

Karen, who brought her lunch to save money, wove her way through the throng until she found Lori and Elaine sitting together and joined them.

"Isn't this a madhouse?" Elaine gestured at the milling hordes of students around them. The cafeteria had originally been a gymnasium, and the basketball hoops still stood at either end. As they watched, an empty milk carton went soaring through one.

"I can hardly hear myself think," Karen admitted.

Lori set aside the yogurt she was eating and leaned across the table. "Elaine was telling me about your tarot cards."

"Oh, those." Karen pulled her tuna sandwich out of its plastic wrapping. "I still need to study them some more."

"Would you mind telling my fortune?" Lori asked, blushing at her own boldness.

"Sure." Karen took a sip of juice. "Actually, I could use the practice. And, well"—she hesitated—"Could I ask a favor in return?"

"Of course." Lori gazed at her over a spoonful of yogurt.

"I wondered if you and Elaine could give me some advice about clothes," Karen said. "I'm, well, trying to change my image."

She felt Lori's gaze sweep instinctively down to Karen's clothes. As usual, she was wearing a wrap-around skirt with a simple blouse, because they were easy to make.

"Lori's great on makeovers. She sure helped me." Elaine split open a package of Twinkies and offered to share them, but Karen and Lori declined. Not everybody could be tall and naturally skinny like Elaine.

"I don't have much money," Karen added quickly. "Actually, I make most of my clothes."

"Me, too." Lori was studying her thoughtfully. "You've got a good figure, Karen, and lovely coloring, but people like you and me have to be careful."

"Why?" Karen asked, feeling a little startled.

"Well, people who have dark, vivid coloring can wear almost anything," Lori explained, pointing across the cafeteria to where Alex Enomoto, who was half-Japanese, had just walked in with her foster sister, Stephanie, also a brunette. "Either one of them could wear a checkered tablecloth and look great."

"But not us?" Karen was beginning to realize how little she knew about fashion.

"That's right." Lori nodded. "Maybe we could go look at fabrics together."

To Karen's delight, the three of them decided on a shopping trip to the mall on Thursday, the first day they were all free.

"We can go to my house afterwards and tell fortunes," Karen suggested.

At that moment, Alex and Stephanie burst upon them, having completed the obstacle course of outstretched legs, slippery floors and misplaced chairs.

"Boy, am I disgusted!" Alex announced as she sat down. "I got up at five o'clock this morning to practice a new dive, and I didn't get it right once. Not once!"

Alex was the champion of the Glenwood High diving team. Everybody knew she was taking aim at the Olympics.

"That dive doesn't know what's good for it," Stephanie observed drily. "It ought to give in gracefully before you pound it into submission."

Stephanie had certainly changed since she transferred to Glenwood High, Karen thought. She remembered the first time she'd seen her, with her dark hair, delicate face, and wary eyes.

There'd been an air of toughness about Stephanie, as if she were the kind of girl who ran around with motorcycle gangs. But then Stephanie had started dating Rick Forrester, one of the richest guys in town but also one of the nicest. Since then, she'd begun to open up more, and Karen realized that the toughness had just been a pose.

"Every time I try to dive, I get water up my nose," Karen admitted. "I guess I'm not much of an athlete."

"Me, either," Lori said.

The bell rang, sending Lori, Elaine, and Karen scurrying to class.

Karen wished they could have talked longer. More than anything, she wanted to talk about Jeff. That funny way Jeff looked at her sometimes . . . but, well, it probably didn't mean anything anyway.

For some odd reason, she found herself wishing it had meant something.

Chapter Nine

After school, Karen joined the other Social Service Committee members in the civics classroom.

Gayle Rodgers gave a report on decorations and publicity for their fund-raising event. A notice was going to come out in the school paper, and posters would go up tomorrow.

Ms. O'Neill came up with some good ideas for activities, including a dance contest with two passes to the movies as first prize.

"I've arranged to borrow a couple of other computers, so we should have a good video games booth," Jeff told them. "And Karen's found her true calling. She must have been a Gypsy in her former life."

Several kids laughed.

"Jeff's just mad because I read his cards and found out he was a pig farmer in *his* last life," Karen retorted, fighting to stay even. The kids chuckled at her remark, too.

As soon as the meeting was over, she hurried out of the building and toward Gennaro's Pizza to avoid any chance of having to walk with Jeff. Facing him at the restaurant was as much as she could handle.

As she strode along, Karen reflected how yesterday, at the park, it had seemed as if things might be changing between them. They'd been able to talk seriously and enjoy themselves together. And then she remembered Jeff's comment today. Obviously, nothing had changed after all.

Would she ever learn not to trust him? she wondered, remembering an old folk saying: Fool me once, shame on you; fool me twice, shame on me.

Karen was tired of being fooled.

When Karen walked into Gennaro's, there were no other customers, just Kit standing behind the counter looking cute. She and her boyfriend, Justin, worked there together.

"Hi," Karen said, glad to see a friendly face. She walked over to the counter. "I'll have a Diet Pepsi, I guess."

"Okay." Kit pulled out a glass and dipped it into the ice compartment. "Hey, I'm really looking forward to the fair on Monday. Everybody's talking about what a great fortune-teller you're going to be."

"Who, me?" Karen wondered for a panicky moment if she was going to end up with the unwanted role of Glenwood's resident psychic.

"Well, I think people are always interested in their own destinies—and in hearing about themselves," Kit said. "And fortune-telling is just one way of getting to hear someone talk about yourself." Karen laughed and took her soft drink from Kit. At that moment Jeff came in.

"Have you told Jeff's fortune yet?" Kit asked. When Karen shook her head, she added mischievously, "Better watch out, then, if you do—you might find yourself a big part of his future." Before Karen could reply, Jeff joined her at the counter and ordered a small pizza. As Kit disappeared into the kitchen, he guided Karen over to a booth, and they sat down.

"Well?" she said, hoping her feigned coolness would offset the way her heart was racing. What had Kit meant by that comment?

"Well, what?" Jeff sipped at his soft drink.

"Well, what did you want to talk about?" Karen asked.

"Oh." He flushed, almost guiltily. "About our parents, of course."

"I know that," Karen said with exaggerated patience. "But what about them? I mean, I tried my best."

"Yeah, I know, things didn't go so well for me either." He rested his arms on the table and stared at his hands. "I talked Dad into jogging with me and talking a cold shower afterwards. I figured he'd be wiped out for the rest of the evening, but he said it invigorated him."

"You don't think they've figured out what we're up to, do you?" Karen asked.

"No." Jeff looked up as Kit called his name. "I don't think my dad would take it too well. He'd probably scream bloody murder."

Karen watched as Jeff crossed the room to pick up his pizza. He'd worn a nice pair of corduroys instead of jeans and a polo shirt that didn't have a rip in it. The shirt stretched a little across his shoulders. It didn't look bad, kind of sexy, actually—if you could look at Jeff's shoulders objectively, that is.

The pizza smelled great, and Karen accepted when Jeff offered her a slice.

"I'll have to come up with something that requires my mom's attention, so Fred can't take her place again," Karen said. "Maybe a sick animal or something."

Jeff screwed up his mouth thoughtfully. "Yeah. I suppose if I keep Dad jogging, eventually he'll run out of steam. Maybe it's a delayed effect."

The door to the pizza shop opened, and Elaine came in with Alex. They didn't notice Karen and Jeff at first as they went over to joke with Kit. As usual, Alex looked as if she were bursting with energy.

"I hope your father doesn't turn out to be like Alex," Karen murmured. "I think she could run a marathon and barely be warmed up."

"No, Dad's always been the smoke-a-pipe-and-sit-by-the-fire type," Jeff said. "Maybe that's why he took the divorce so hard. He really misses having a home and family."

"He does have a home and family!" Karen protested. "You!"

"It's not the same." Jeff's voice had an unhappy edge to it. "I really tried, though. You should have seen me trying to cook hot dogs for the first time when I was eight—I wanted to surprise my dad by making dinner. But, what a disaster! I boiled them for half an hour, and they swelled up till they looked like they'd been dead for a week."

"Yuck." Karen made a face. "I should think you'd *want* your dad to get married again."

"Oh, I've learned to cook a lot better since then," Jeff assured her. "But my memories of the family at dinner together aren't exactly the best, either. When my parents were married, they used to fight at the dinner table. My stomach churned so much I could hardly eat."

"That must have been awful," Karen sympathized, feeling strangely unhungry herself.

"Yeah," Jeff agreed. "I remember one time my mom was yelling at Dad that she was going to take us kids and leave — go as far away as she could get, like maybe Alaska. My sister and I looked at each other, and it was as if somebody'd given a signal. We both puked at the same time."

Karen stared at her half-eaten slice of pizza, fighting the urge to get up and go put her arms around Jeff. "I can see how a person could lose their appetite."

Elaine spotted Karen and came over. "I hope I'm not interrupting," she said. "I just wanted to say hi."

She glanced at Jeff, and Karen felt herself blushing. This must look like a date, she realized. "We were just discussing the Social Service fair," she said quickly.

Alex waved from across the room. "Hi, guys! Hey, come on, Elaine, do you want pepperoni or mushrooms?"

"What's the difference?" Elaine said. "At Gennaro's, they taste the same."

Behind them, Kit laughed, then looked around to be sure her boss hadn't overheard.

After Elaine returned to the counter, Karen glanced at Jeff, wondering how she'd feel if this really were a date. He was frowning to himself as he ate, momentarily lost in thought.

What would they talk about on a date? she wondered. So far, their conversations consisted of either insulting each other or conspiring on Operation Split.

It has hard to imagine Jeff getting close to a girl. Studying him across the table, Karen suddenly realized why.

Jeff was like her. He joked and teased in order to hide his deeper feelings. The realization rocked her. Jeff was afraid of getting hurt, just as she was! So what would a date with him be like?

Karen imagined Jeff driving up in his father's car to pick her up. She would answer the door and see him standing there looking handsome in some new khakis and a soft cotton shirt that would bring out the blue in his eyes. He'd look at her admiringly, taking in her dress (it would be a new one, made with Lori's advice), and then he'd say something romantic like "Hey, you forgot to put a potato sack over your head."

Karen sighed.

"Maybe I'd better go." Jeff had finished the last of his pizza. "Karen, just promise me one thing."

"What's that?"

"That you're serious about this." His gaze met hers straight on. "That you're honestly doing your best at Operation Split; you're not just pretending."

"Of course I'm serious! Why would I pretend?"

He shrugged. "I don't know. Maybe as a joke."

"Well, you certainly deserve it!" Karen still smarted from his crack in the committee meeting. "But I'm not like that. Besides, I want what's best for my mom, and judging from what you've said about him, I'm sure it isn't your father!"

"Okay. And Karen . . ." He hesitated as if about to add something important. Then he mumbled, "Thanks."

Karen watched Jeff go, torn between wanting to give him a hug and wanting to throw her Pepsi glass at his head.

She'd forgotten about Elaine and Alex until they slid into the booth opposite her, bringing their pizza.

"So Captain Kid is warming up," Elaine said, selecting a piece piled high with mushrooms. "I'm glad to see you guys are getting along better."

"Don't be too sure of that." Karen watched out the window as Jeff's figure disappeared down the street. "You never know with Jeff."

"It's obvious he likes you," Alex stated. "He's always hanging around you."

"Kind of like a housefly?" Karen laughed.

"Oh, I think he's cute." Elaine smiled. "And so do you."

That was the one problem with Elaine—she was too observant.

"He's all right," Karen said, "except for his personality."

They invited Alex to come shopping with them on Thursday, but she had diving practice. So instead, they agreed to get together at Elaine's the following Wednesday night.

"Maybe you could read Stephanie's fortune," Alex

suggested. "She's really nervous about meeting her mother." She folded her slice of pizza in half and practically inhaled it. With all the energy she used up, Alex never needed to worry about calories.

"Meeting her mother?" Karen knew that Alex's family had taken in Stephanie as their foster daughter after Alex's younger brother, Noodle, died of cystic fibrosis, but she didn't know anything about Stephanie's past.

"Her mom abandoned her when she was five," Alex explained. "She's got a lead on her mother's whereabouts, and she's excited about it, but she's nervous, too."

"I should think so," Karen said, amazed at Alex's matter-of-factness.

"Yeah, and if you did, it would probably just make her even more nervous," Alex admitted.

Raindrops splattered against the window, and Karen groaned. "Oh, no. I'm going to get soaked."

"Don't worry." Alex grinned. "I'll give you a ride home if you don't mind the Green Demon."

"Are you kidding? If a car isn't a clunker, I'm scared to get in it," Karen joked.

Riding home in the rain in Alex's old car, the three of them sang the words of an old camp song, *It Was Sad When the Great Ship Went Down*, with Alex supplying a contralto for "to the bottom of the..." while Elaine and Karen chipped in with "husbands and wives..." in their off-key sopranos.

Karen arrived home, feeling recharged and carefree.

Even if Jeff didn't care about her, it was nice to have friends who did.

Chapter Ten

Anne worked late at the clinic on Tuesday, but Wednesday night, immediately after dinner, she changed into a flattering emerald sweater and gray linen pants.

Obviously she had a date with Mr. Becker.

Karen sat on her bed chewing her nails. She simply had to come up with something.

Her glance fell on Perri the squirrel, who was stirring restlessly in his cage. As Karen watched, he began gnawing vigorously at the cast on his leg.

That gave her an idea.

"Mom!" Karen hurried into her mother's bedroom. "I think something's wrong with Perri."

"What is it?" Anne was applying mascara to her already thick lashes, something she hardly ever did.

"Well..." Karen hedged, her mind racing. "He... um, was twitching around earlier and now he's chewing like mad on his cast. I think it's hurting him."

"I'll change it tomorrow," Anne promised.

"But, Mom, I'm kind of worried," Karen persisted, noticing at the same time how beautiful her mother looked. Once again she felt a wave of guilt. The last thing she wanted was to hurt Anne.

"Well, let me see." Her mother smiled at her warmly and went to look at Perri.

"Hmm." Heedless of her good pants, Anne knelt on the floor and examined the squirrel. "He is worrying it, isn't he? They're such little creatures, the least problem can carry them off."

"Yeah, that's what I was thinking. He'll probably drive himself crazy tonight if we don't do something."

"I'll tell you what." Her mother stood up. "Art's working at the clinic until nine. Why don't you take Perri over there? I'm sure he won't mind."

Karen's heart sank, but before she could think of an objection, her mother was gone.

"Oh, great," she muttered to herself as she lugged the cage down the stairs. Not only had she failed to break up the date, she'd also saddled herself with a trip to the clinic.

On the other hand, maybe Perri really was having problems.

The clinic was housed in a low tan building on a side street near the downtown area. As she pulled into the parking lot, Karen noticed half a dozen other cars there.

In the doorway, she paused for a moment, inhaling the familiar fragrance. The clinic smelled of a combination of disinfectant and animals—a clean, oddly reassuring scent, like a stable.

Looking around the brightly decorated orange-and-tan waiting room, Karen thought about how much this place meant to her mother. For the first year or so after Dad died, Anne had rarely smiled, but getting involved with her work had really helped her deal with her grief. Art was a great and very supportive partner. Together they'd made a terrific success of the clinic.

But today something was wrong. The receptionist's desk was empty, and Karen realized there was no one to assist the people sitting impatiently with their dogs and cats.

Karen walked between a row of tan upholstered benches to the sturdy oak desk. She set the squirrel cage in the corner where the dogs and cats would be less likely to notice it and asked the people to tell her who was next in line.

By the time Art was ready for the next patient, she'd organized the area and listed each of the clients in order.

Then she took the ledger from a desk drawer and began updating it from a stack of receipts, copying down the figures with a sharp pencil. The bank took care of the major billing and balancing of the accounts, but day-to-day receipts had to be entered. Karen shook her head as she saw that the secretary was over a week behind.

"Boy, am I glad to see you," Art told her in a low voice when he emerged a few minutes later. Even in his white vet's smock, the older man looked distinguished with his head of silver hair and matching thick mustache.

Karen explained about Perri, then added, "Where's the receptionist?"

"She's been sick, but we wanted to hold her job open for her," Art explained, "although that may not be possible. We've been using a series of temporary workers, but you know how that is. They do their best, but they don't know where things are, and they also don't like to work evenings and weekends."

Karen ended up staying until closing time. Noticing that charts and notes were stacked haphazardly on the desk and the file cabinet, she began putting them away. In between, she made out bills for each of the clients as they came out and put their cash and checks carefully in the cashbox.

A little over an hour later, after Art had finally tended to Perri and removed the squirrel's cast, Karen prepared to go.

"Thanks again for all your help," Art said as he flexed Perri's leg carefully. "As you can see, the office is a mess."

"It really is," Karen agreed.

"I don't suppose..." Art hesitated.

"What?" she asked absently as she fed Perri some rabbit food to quiet him.

"If by any chance you were free on Saturdays..." Art continued. "It's almost impossible to find a receptionist to work weekends, and we could sure use the help. Plus I noticed you made a start on the filing. I can't tell you how much I appreciate that."

What could she say? Karen knew how hard her mother worked to make a living. Several times Karen had suggested getting an after-school job, but Anne wouldn't hear of it.

The least she could do was help out at the clinic.

"Sure, I'd be delighted," she told Art. "And thanks for fixing up Perri."

Driving home and reflecting on how badly her plan had gone awry, Karen smiled ruefully. Operation Split was rapidly turning into a comedy of errors.

The next day on the way to the mall, Elaine and Lori coaxed her to tell them the whole story behind Operation Split.

"You really want to split them up?" Lori asked. "What if they're in love?"

Karen was beginning to wonder that herself. "Then I guess I'm doomed to failure."

Once they arrived, Karen started to head for the fabric shop, but Lori stopped her.

"I think you should try things on in Macy's first," she recommended. "That way you can see how the different colors actually look on you."

"That's right," Elaine agreed.

Karen was surprised to find that the bright greens she loved didn't look nearly as good on her as they did on her mother. In fact, staring at her reflection in the mirror, she had to admit that the green sheath dress she wore was not particularly flattering. "I look like a mixed-up carrot that got its colors reversed."

White, which she usually chose for blouses, made her skin look muddy. "Yecch." Karen pulled off the shirt she was trying on. "I'm beginning to think this is a hopeless cause. How come I never noticed before how awful this stuff looks?"

"It doesn't look awful," Elaine protested loyally.

"Just—bland."

Lori glided back into the dressing booth with another armload of clothes. She looked indignant. "That saleslady counted these clothes twice, as if she were afraid I'd steal something."

"At these prices, they're the ones who're stealing," Elaine remarked.

Karen listened, enthralled, as Lori explained that the key to a coordinated wardrobe was deciding which neutral colors to use.

"The most common combinations are navy and white, black and gray or brown and natural," she explained, handing Karen an off-white blouse she had picked off the rack. Karen was startled to see how much more flattering the color was on her than pure white.

Beginning to feel excited, she tried on dress after dress, discovering that brown and natural—which she'd never particularly liked—actually looked good with her vivid red coloring.

Light green turned out to be flattering, too, and so did orange, a color Karen had always avoided.

"Talk about fortune-tellers!" she teased Lori. "You're the one who's a magician!"

Finally they adjourned to the fabric store, where they picked out lengths of material and some patterns that Lori said would make Karen look taller.

"Have you ever thought about going into fashion design?" she asked Lori. "Of course, you'd make a great model, but that could be boring after a while."

"Yes, I know. After I've made my first couple of million, I'll have to find something else more challenging." Lori giggled. Then, in a more serious tone, she added, "Sure I've thought about it, but I really love the idea of being a model. I just don't know if I'm pretty enough."

"Wouldn't you know it? The most gorgeous girl in Glenwood, and she can't figure it out." Elaine made a face, and Karen couldn't help laughing.

When they got back to the Waverlys', Karen noted with relief that neither Zack nor Fred was home.

She fixed a snack of vegetables with yogurt dip. Lori was always on a diet, and Karen decided she wouldn't mind losing a few pounds herself to look good in the new clothes she was going to make.

Among the patterns was one for a dress with a medieval flair. If she worked hard, she could have it done by the weekend in time for the fair.

Would Jeff notice? Karen visualized a scene from the old movies, where the secretary whips off her glasses and the hero's eyes fly open in amazement.

No, she couldn't picture Jeff doing that. He'd make some smart-aleck remark instead.

The three girls adjourned to Karen's bedroom. It was funny how much she missed Perri's familiar rustling, but she'd released the squirrel that morning after making sure his leg was fully healed.

Karen got out her cards. After shuffling the cards carefully, she laid out Lori's fortune. Just as they were getting to some good questions about the future and Lori's romantic life, Zack tapped at the door and stepped inside without waiting for an invitation. "I heard voices and thought I'd better come and investigate — in case it was a bunch of female burglars."

Karen introduced him to Lori. Zack exchanged a

few polite comments, but he couldn't keep his eyes off Elaine.

"I didn't know you were home." Elaine's words sounded calm enough, but her face glowed.

"We just got here." He leaned in the doorway, regarding the tarot cards. "What are you doing?"

"I'm practicing for a fair we're having at school Monday," Karen explained, gathering the cards. "I'm supposed to be the fortune-teller."

"How about telling mine?" Zack asked.

She couldn't very well refuse, so she asked him for a yes-or-no question.

"Okay." He sat on the floor next to Elaine. Most guys would have been embarrassed about joining in with a group of girls, Karen thought, but Zack seemed right at home. "Let's see. How about—will I be lucky in love?"

Lori, who hadn't missed what had just passed between Elaine and Zack, blushed furiously, and even Elaine looked mildly embarrassed. Karen was torn between amusement and annoyance. Zack certainly had more than enough self-confidence!

She spread out the cards. The one that represented the future was the Four of Pentacles reversed. The card showed a seated man hugging tight to his possessions. Upside down, it meant delay.

"Looks like you're not going to get an answer anytime soon," Karen interpreted.

"Oh, well, I'm a patient man." Zack got up, winked at Elaine, and left.

"He's cute," Lori whispered.

Elaine smiled, then glanced at her watch. "Oh, gosh, it's almost dinnertime. I'd better get going."

"Me, too," Lori agreed. "Mom had an important court case today, and that always means she'll be starving when she gets home."

Lori's mother, Karen had heard, was a lot like Anne. A lawyer, she took on clients she cared about even if they couldn't pay.

Zack had already started dinner by the time Lori and Elaine left. Karen wandered into the kitchen and watched him stirring the spaghetti into a pot of boiling water. Her brother could be maddening, but at times, like now, she realized how considerate he was.

When their mother got home, she was full of compliments for Karen. "Art said you were terrific last night, honey. And I really appreciate your offering to help on Saturdays."

Fred, who had come downstairs for dinner, gave Karen an approving look. "That was nice of you. As a matter of fact, I've been wondering if I could help out next summer, Mom."

"You mean you're not going to spend all summer buried in your room?" Anne teased.

He ducked his head. "I guess I have been overdoing it. Actually, I thought it might be good for me to assist at your surgeries, if you don't mind. If I'm going to be a doctor, I'd better get used to the sight of blood."

Dinner was a time when the Waverlys shared the events of the day. As Karen looked around the table at the happy faces of her family, she thought about Jeff's parents, fighting so much their kids couldn't eat. She felt a pang for her nemesis and wondered if he'd ever experienced the kind of happiness she'd grown so accustomed to.

"You missed Karen's hen party." At Zack's words, her ears perked up. "Did you know she's taken up fortune-telling?"

"No, really?" Anne turned toward her daughter.

Karen explained about the fair. "I'm not very good at it, but Lori and Elaine let me practice on them."

"Don't forget me," Zack admonished. "I'm the one who has to wait for my wish. Isn't that what you said?"

"Oh, what fun!" Anne said enthusiastically. "I've always wanted to have my fortune told. Would you mind, Karen?"

"No, of course not, I'd love to." Maybe the tarot cards would keep her mother's thoughts off romance.

It was a vain hope. Almost immediately, Anne added, "You wouldn't object to doing Mr. Becker's, too, would you? I'll go give him a call right now."

Karen was left with her mouth open as her mother got up from the table.

As fate—or just plain luck—would have it, Mr. Becker was indeed free that evening and, Anne announced joyfully, would join them shortly.

She hurried upstairs to change, leaving Karen and her brothers to clean up.

"You really don't like the idea of Mom getting serious about a man, do you?" Fred asked as he scrubbed a pot. Since Zack had done most of the cooking, they'd excused him from cleanup duty.

"Well"—Karen sponged off the stove top—"Mostly I don't want Jeff Becker to be my stepbrother. He's so obnoxious, I wouldn't feel comfortable in my own home."

"I suspect you'd get used to him," Fred decided. "Besides, we'd be three against one."

"Yeah—three boys against one girl." Karen shot him a teasing look.

He grinned back, looking more like the easygoing Fred he'd been before Kathy left. "Only if you deserve it."

"What's going on?" she asked as she dried the pot. "You seem more relaxed than usual."

"Who knows?" He shrugged. "A guy gets tired of grinding away all the time."

The doorbell rang, and Karen went to answer it.

Mr. Becker looked the way she remembered him. He was about Jeff's height, wearing dark-rimmed glasses and a serious expression. But she'd never paid close enough attention before to notice the bright blue of his eyes behind the lenses or the shy way he had of hunching his shoulders.

"Hi," she said.

"Hello, Karen." He stepped inside. "So, I hear you're turning into Glenwood's Jeanne Dixon."

"It's just for fun," she explained.

Her mother came downstairs, and Karen went to get the cards and a soda for herself. They settled at the dining room table, the three of them and Fred. Zack had disappeared—probably to talk on the telephone with Elaine, Karen thought.

Anne was reluctant to ask a yes-or-no question. "Can't you guess what I want to ask?" she finally said, and Karen had to bite her tongue to keep from groaning.

"Well, okay."

The cards were a mixture of ups and downs, end-

102

ings and beginnings. Karen couldn't make much sense of them, but one fact was obvious: the card representing the future was that of the Lovers.

"Of course, it could refer to any kind of love — the love of your family, for instance," she cautioned her mother, but clearly her warning was useless.

"Now it's Albert's turn." Anne beamed at Mr. Becker, who wiped his glasses on his handkerchief as if they'd suddenly gotten misted over.

It's a good thing you can't see us now, Jeff, Karen thought, miserably.

As it turned out, Mr. Becker's fortune was just as bad — from Karen's point of view. Most of his cards referred to caution, which was obviously one of his prominent characteristics, but his outcome card, the Four of Wands, showed two women lifting bouquets of flowers beneath a canopy. What could that mean? Suddenly Karen realized with horror that it looked like a wedding celebration!

The last sip of Coke she'd taken went down the wrong way, and Karen erupted into a fit of coughing and choking. Zack pounded her on the back, and after a moment the fit subsided. Quickly Karen scooped up the cards before she could do any more damage.

"Oh, sweetheart, thank you," her mother said.

"Yes, that was very interesting." Mr. Becker cleared his throat. "Very amusing."

"Oh, gee. Well, thanks for letting me practice on you. But don't take any of this too seriously," she urged them.

Fred merely eyed her knowingly. Impulsively, she said, "Do you want yours done, too?"

He shook his head. "No. I think I'll let the future take care of itself."

A few minutes later, passing by the living room, Karen noticed her mother and Mr. Becker sitting side by side on the couch, holding hands.

"Isn't it funny about the cards?" Anne was saying.

Karen trudged up the stairs to her room, feeling like a condemned woman. Jeff was going to kill her.

Chapter Eleven

"That was wonderful, just wonderful," Jeff snarled. "You should have seen my father. He came home whistling! It seems a certain redheaded double-crosser told him he was going to get married and live happily ever after!"

Karen glared at him, stung by the accusation that she'd deliberately sabotaged things. "I should think you'd be glad to see your father feeling good!"

"That's easy for you to say. You're not going to have to pick up the pieces afterwards!" She'd never seen Jeff so angry before.

They were sitting at the picnic table in the grove, a secluded circle of trees above the high school football field. It was a place that had always been special to Karen, a warm, safe spot to talk to Betsy or just sit and think with no one else around.

Now the afternoon breeze cut straight through the trees, chilling her despite her light jacket. As if that weren't enough, Jeff was radiating pure ice.

"In case you're interested, I didn't do it on purpose," Karen defended herself. "I was hoping to keep my mother busy by telling her fortune."

"It didn't occur to you things might backfire?"

"You seem to forget, I'm a fortune-teller, not a mind reader," Karen snapped. "By the way, just remember whose idea it was that I tell fortunes in the first place."

Jeff stood up and paced alongside the picnic table. He looked a little thin, she noticed, and wondered if he was still eating overcooked hot dogs for dinner.

"I thought I could count on you." He turned to face her. "I thought you wanted to help."

"I did!" She wished tears weren't burning behind her eyelids. Why should she care if Jeff misjudged her? "It's not my fault everything I do turns out wrong. Operation Split was your idea, anyway!"

"Yeah, well, I'm not the one who loused it up." His jaw looked so tight, Karen wondered if he was grinding his teeth.

"Look, I've had enough of your insults!" she cried, clutching her books so tightly her knuckles turned white.

"Then stop deserving them!" he shot over his shoulder as he resumed pacing.

Karen jumped to her feet. "You're the most obnoxious boy I've ever met, Jeff Becker! You never think about anybody but yourself!"

"Hey . . ." He lifted his hands, palms outward, as if to soothe her, but it was too late.

"You don't care about my mother, or me!" She was shouting so loud her throat hurt. "You take every chance you get to put me down. Well, I'm sick of it! Other people have rights around here, too. From now on, you can 'save' your father all by yourself! Just count me out!"

Grabbing her books, Karen stalked through the trees and down across the field. Once she thought she heard her name called, but she didn't turn around.

Tears pricked her eyes as she reached her locker and slammed the books inside. She felt angered and hurt. Just when she thought things had been going well with her and Jeff...well, she should have known better. She'd opened to him once before, and look what happened. Why should it have been any different this time?

The only other person around was Alex Enomoto, her wet hair a testament to her determined diving practice. Anybody else would have stopped to dry it before coming outside, but Alex probably found it hard to stand still that long.

"Must be Jeff Becker," Alex said, seeing Karen's face. "Nobody else can be that infuriating."

Karen forced a laugh to hide her tears. "You mean I'm not the only one who's noticed?"

Alex smiled, her expression sympathetic. "Men always drive you crazy. Hey, you want a ride home?"

"Sure." They walked out to the Green Demon together, but Alex was strangely silent. Her cheerful demeanor had suddenly vanished, and Karen couldn't help wondering if something was wrong. In some ways, Alex seemed like the most resilient person at Glenwood High. A bundle of energy, she was not only an excellent athlete but strikingly good-looking, too, with her dark hair and almond-shaped eyes.

Yet Karen knew that Alex's brother had died only a short time ago, and soon afterwards, Alex had broken up with her longtime boyfriend, Danny. In addition, there'd been her new foster sister, Stephanie, to deal with; and Stephanie must have been hard to take at first, until she got over her tough-girl pose.

"Are you okay?" Karen asked after they'd been driving for a while.

"Oh" — Alex shook her head a little, as if she'd been daydreaming — "I guess you know I've been dating a guy, Wes Thorsen — he's a race car driver."

Karen had heard something about it, but not being a racing fan, she didn't know much about Wes. "Right," she said.

"I've decided to break up with him." Alex stared straight ahead as she slowed for a stoplight. "It's just too much. The last wreck he was in — visiting him in the hospital — it reminded me of losing Noodle. I can't take it."

"I don't blame you," Karen said sympathetically. Then she thought about Jeff and how she kept hoping that he'd change no matter how badly or unreasonably he acted. Was she in a self-destructive pattern just like Alex? "But knowing something intellectually doesn't always make it easier, does it?" she added.

"I guess not." Alex's dark eyes looked unhappy. "Sometimes it feels as if things never work out the way I want them to."

"Maybe that's part of the trick, learning to want what you get when you don't get what you want,"

Karen said.

She found herself picturing her mother. Mom's life certainly hadn't been easy, losing her beloved husband, raising three children alone, working hard and never having a penny to spare. Yet she'd always seemed happy enough.

Why had Karen been so eager to break up her mother's romance? She was glad now that Operation Split hadn't worked. Anne deserved a loving husband, and if it meant Karen would have to put up with Jeff living in the house...Well, she just couldn't think about that. Not right now, anyway.

They rode the rest of the way in silence. As they pulled up to Karen's house, Alex said, "You're going to be at Elaine's on Wednesday, aren't you?"

Karen had almost forgotten about the get-together. "Oh, sure."

"Great. See you then." Alex let her out and, with a wave, gunned off.

Karen walked slowly into the house. She wasn't looking forward to the weekend. She wished it were Monday night instead and that the fair were already over. She'd had enough of telling fortunes to last her a lifetime.

Chapter Twelve

On Saturday, Karen worked most of the day at the clinic, digging through piles of paperwork and sneezing from the dust.

Despite her weariness, she spent Saturday night sewing her medieval-style gown, a russet-colored dress with a high waist and full sleeves inset with orange. Lori assured her she'd look fabulous in it, and Karen knew the outfit would be perfect for her fortune-telling.

She and her mother baked some bread and played Scrabble on Sunday morning, but that afternoon Anne had a date. Around four o'clock, Karen wandered into her mother's room and, perched on a dressing room chair, watched as Anne put on make-up and perfume.

"I wish I looked like you." Karen sighed as Anne brushed out her auburn hair, seated in front of the pearl-gray Art Deco vanity table.

"Why?" Her mother turned in surprise. "You're cute.'"

"But—uncoordinated." Karen plucked at the blue-green blouse she'd thrown on this morning without thinking about how it clashed with her pants. "Do you think the things Lori suggested will really make a difference? I mean, everything looks great when she wears it—but that's because she's got this knack."

"You should have seen me when I was a teenager," Anne said, shaking her head and accidentally smudging the mascara she'd been so carefully applying. "And as for being uncoordinated, I think it's a family trait."

"Yes, but—even when you don't try, you have a kind of natural elegance," Karen pointed out.

Anne chuckled as she wiped the mascara off with a tissue, the last one in the box. "When everybody else was wearing Jackie Kennedy suits and pillbox hats, I was wearing stained jeans and ripped T-shirts, chasing a wounded possum under the house or rescuing puppies someone had thrown out of a car."

Karen brought in another box of Kleenex from the adjacent bathroom. "How did you manage to get all grown-up?"

Anne smiled. "It sort of sneaks up on you."

"Like love?" Karen sat on the edge of the bed. "Does love sneak up on you?"

Anne paused. "I guess it does," she replied thoughtfully.

"Are you in love with Mr. Becker?" Karen held her breath.

"It's a bit early to tell," her mother said with a smile. She began to apply lipstick, carefully following the contours of her full mouth.

Karen decided not to press the subject. The last thing she wanted was to give her mother ideas! "Where are you going tonight?"

"Out for dinner. Unless you have another one of your 'emergencies,'" Anne teased.

Karen turned a fiery red. Their eyes met in the mirror, and Anne turned around in her seat. "I was just joking," she marveled. "Do you mean you were doing it on purpose?"

There was no need to answer. The truth was obvious. "Mom, I didn't mean..." Karen didn't know how to explain.

"Oh, Karen" — her mother turned to face her — "are you really upset about my dating? I didn't think you minded."

"I don't," Karen protested, feeling like a total creep. Instead of getting mad, her mom was acting sympathetic, and that was even worse. "I just — well, I don't want Jeff Becker as a stepbrother."

"'Stepbrother?'" Anne's eyebrows lifted in amazement. "Honey, I've only gone out with Albert for a few weeks. I hadn't even thought about getting married."

"Yes, but..." Karen sputtered, wishing she'd never agreed to go along with Jeff's idiotic Operation Split. "Well, I think you should do whatever will make you happy, Mom."

Anne gave her a hug. "I want us all to be happy."

After her mother left for her date, Karen sank onto the living room sofa. She felt rotten. How could she

112

have schemed against the person she loved most in the world?

A screech of brakes on the street outside startled her. Then came a twisted yowl, the sound of an animal in terrible pain. Dashing to the window, Karen looked out just in time to see a green car speeding away.

In the middle of the street lay a small, furry lump. Garfield! Her heart pounding in her throat, Karen raced outside and into the street. It *was* Garfield—he was still alive, but barely.

She knelt in the street and cradled the furry body in her arms, oblivious of the hot tears that burned down her cheeks. He must be in such terrible pain! If only she were a vet like her mother and knew exactly what to do! She couldn't bear to lose him, but if she didn't do something fast, her pet would die. That thought pushed Karen into action.

Carrying the cat to the shelter of the house, she laid him on the softest thing she could find, an old wool sweater from the front closet. Garfield lifted his head weakly and met her gaze, blinking twice before laying his head back down. Karen felt as if her heart were being torn out of her body.

Fred and Zack had gone to a movie, so no one else was home.

Dashing to the front hall, Karen grabbed the telephone. Her mother was out with Mr. Becker, so maybe they were over at his house. Her trembling fingers kept slipping on the old-fashioned rotary dial. Karen had to try the number three times before she completed the call.

It rang once, twice. Oh, please let them be home,

she prayed.

Somebody picked up the phone. "Hello?" It was Jeff.

"Jeff? This is Karen." Her voice was shaking, but at the reassuring sound of his voice, she suddenly forgot how angry she'd been at him. "Is my mother there?"

"No, they went out to eat," Jeff said. "Is something wrong?"

Karen told him about Garfield. Without warning, she burst into tears again. "I don't know what to do. Jeff, he's going to die!"

"No, he isn't." Jeff sounded strong and dependable. "What about your mother's partner? Is he at the clinic today?"

"They're closed on Sunday. But there's an answering service. He should be on call." Karen knew her mother and Art alternated carrying a beeper, but they rarely got emergency calls, and it was possible he'd forgotten to turn it on.

"You call him, and I'll bring the car over," Jeff instructed, taking charge.

Fortunately, Art was home, and when he heard the situation he promised to meet Karen and Jeff at the clinic.

Jeff arrived while Karen was still on the phone. He insisted on carrying Garfield out to the car himself and settling the cat gently in Karen's arms. Even so, the slam of the car door made the cat twitch, and Karen's heart turned over at his suffering.

"I can't believe this is happening!" She didn't even care that she was crying as Jeff pulled away from the curb. She looked down at the furry bundle cradled in her arms. "He's such a smart cat. He knows about cars. How could he have gotten hit?"

"People get hit sometimes, too, and they certainly know about safety. Maybe the car just came around the corner too fast." They stopped for a red light, and Jeff reached over to touch Garfield's fur. "He seems to be breathing regularly."

"Can't you hear how he's wheezing?" Karen cried. "Maybe his ribs punctured his lungs or something."

"Cats are pretty resilient," Jeff said soothingly. He shifted the car into first gear and then quickly to third, maneuvering through the streets as fast as the speed limit would allow. "They don't have nine lives for nothing."

Karen was touched by his effort to reassure her, and she tried to be brave. Still, she'd never known the trip to the clinic could take so long. It felt like hours before they halted in the parking lot.

Art's van pulled up right behind them. "Let's get that patient on the operating table," he said, springing up the steps and unlocking the clinic's front door.

After settling Garfield in the surgery room, Karen and Jeff washed up. Upset as she was, Karen knew Art could work faster if he had someone to hand him the bandages and equipment he needed. But all her good intentions fell apart as she held Garfield and watched Art approach with a needleful of anesthetic.

The cat saw him coming, too. Garfield had been "fixed," and he knew the needle was going to hurt. He began to whimper pitifully, a sound that went right to Karen's heart.

She burst into tears all over again. "He trusts me! I can't stand here and let you hurt him. I know you have to, but he doesn't understand!"

"I'll do it." Without jarring the cat, Jeff gently lifted Garfield from Karen's arms and clucked reassuringly as Art inserted the needle. Garfield meowed again, with only a ghost of his usual spunk. His tail twitched for a moment, and then he was asleep.

"There are a couple of broken bones," Art said. "But it's the internal injuries I'm worried about—internal bleeding."

It seemed to take hours while he probed and cut and splinted and bandaged. Several times Karen felt as if she were going to faint, but Jeff's strong arm around her steadied her. She felt so glad to have him there! By the time Art was finished, Garfield looked like a miniature Egyptian mummy with ears.

"I wish we had a twenty-four-hour infirmary, but I'm sure you'll do a good job of taking care of him," Art said. "I'm going to give him another shot, and he should sleep soundly for a while."

They borrowed a cat bed and transferred the snoozing Garfield to the car.

"Art, I don't know how to thank you," Karen said as he turned toward his van.

The veterinarian reached over and gave Karen a hug. "I'm just glad I was home. We really appreciate all the work you did yesterday. Consider this a token payment."

Jeff didn't drive directly home. When he took a turn that led out of town and up toward the hills, Karen realized she was glad. Somehow she didn't feel like being alone right now.

116

The crisp smell of pine needles wafted through the window. Right outside of town, and you find yourself in the middle of the country, she thought. Through a screen of trees, Karen could see the gentle rolling hills of a vineyard, with young grapevines leafing out on the trellises. A relieved peacefulness settled over her.

"It always makes me feel better to drive through the hills," Jeff murmured, running a hand through his tousled blond hair. It had been a trying hour for him, too, Karen realized.

Karen glanced at the back seat to make sure Garfield was still sleeping soundly. The sight of the little heap of bandages made her feel strangely reassured. She knew he was going to be all right.

"You know we got Garfield at one of these farms," she said. "He was one of a litter of seven, the smallest one. Mom was delivering a calf, and I'd come along to watch. Then this teeny kitten wobbled over, and I fell in love."

"I can see why." Jeff flicked on the car lights as the twilight deepened. "I'm mostly a dog person, but I like Garfield. It's funny how animals get to be like people, isn't it? When Bluto got hurt in that dogfight, I couldn't sleep the next night. Finally I brought hm upstairs to sleep in my room."

"Mom thinks animals *are* like people, and I do, too." Karen rested her head against the back of the seat. "When I saw Garfield lying there in the street, it suddenly brought back all my memories of when Dad died. This big hole opened up inside me."

Jeff nodded. "That's kind of how I felt when my parents split up. Suddenly there was just Dad and me. I went around being afraid that I'd lose him, too."

"So did I!" Karen stared in amazement. "I was so afraid Mom would die, too, and I was afraid to tell anybody. I guess I thought that if I actually said it, that might make it happen."

Jeff pulled over at a view point where they could see across the Palo Alto hills and down to the town below. House lights were flickering on like fireflies in the dusk.

"I used to dream about something like this happening," he said, half to himself.

"What?" Karen was puzzled. "My cat getting hit by a car?"

He chuckled. "No, of course not. But about well . . . I'd daydream about you being attacked by hoodlums, and then I'd come and drive them off."

Karen felt the blood rush to her face. Her heart started to pound. What was he saying? What did he mean by saying that he had fantasized about rescuing her?

"If you wanted me to like you, why did you pick on me all the time?" she asked. "I thought you couldn't stand me."

Jeff looked embarrassed. "You've heard of the old days when if a boy liked a girl, he dipped her braid into the inkwell."

"I'd have poured ink over his head," Karen replied promptly.

"Yeah, I know. You didn't exactly know how to take a hint," Jeff said, but he was looking at her with admiration.

"What about that summer at the beach?" she asked.

Jeff rested one arm along the back of the seat so it brushed lightly against her neck, stirring up an electric current that sizzled through her. "That was fun, wasn't it?"

"Well, I thought so at the time," Karen said. She stared at Jeff, transfixed by his changed tone.

"That barbecue on the beach was great." Jeff's eyes half-closed as he remembered. "You looked cute, like Gidget in those old beach movies."

It felt strange, seeing herself through Jeff's eyes. "I thought maybe I was kind of a nuisance, showing up unexpectedly, and you felt you had to put up with me."

"Why did you think that?" He toyed with a strand of her hair, and Karen felt her breath catch in her throat. She could feel the warmth of his hand near her cheek, and she shivered. "I had a good time," Jeff continued. "It was something I'd hoped would happen, and then suddenly it did, and I could hardly believe it."

Karen listened with increasing amazement. She felt as if she'd fallen through a rabbit hole and the world had turned upside down. Was this really Jeff Becker speaking?

"I enjoyed that week at the beach, too," she said, her voice trembling with hesitation. "I thought..."

The words stuck in her throat.

"Thought what?" Jeff asked.

"Well, afterwards, at the sophomore dance, I thought you'd still be interested in me," Karen said, "but you spent all your time with Meredith Shaw."

When Jeff didn't reply, she added, "Anyway, after that I figured that I'd misjudged the whole thing." To her horror, a tear slipped down her cheek. She hoped Jeff couldn't see it in the gathering dark.

No such luck. "Are you crying?" His arm tightened around her shoulder. "Oh, Karen, I thought—well, you walked in, and you were so cute, and all the boys were looking at you, and I thought maybe if I flirted with Meredith . . ."

"You were trying to make me jealous?" she asked incredulously.

"In a way." Jeff frowned. "It's hard to say exactly. It was kind of like when my mother walked out on me. I loved her so much, and she just left. Just in case you were going to do the same thing, I wanted to show I didn't care."

"But I'm not your mother," she protested.

"Yeah, I noticed." He drew her close against his chest, and she could feel his heart thumping. It seemed incredible, but Jeff obviously felt as nervous as she did.

His fingers stroked her arm, moving up to touch the bare skin of her neck, and the world slowed down. Jeff shifted so that they faced each other. His blue eyes seemed to sparkle with a light of their own in the dusky darkness. He searched her face until he found the answer he was looking for. Then gently, he leaned over and touched his lips to hers.

Karen felt as if she'd been zapped with a thousand volts of electricity. She'd been kissed before, but never like this. She wanted it to go on forever.

His arms encircled her, and they kissed again. Delirious with happiness, Karen forgot where she was. She forgot about what had happened that afternoon, she forgot about everything but Jeff. Nestled in his arms, knowing that he *wanted* her, she knew she was where she belonged.

They sat side by side with her head on his shoulder, gazing out over the hills. Garfield stirred in the back seat, sighed, and went to sleep again.

A warm glow bathed Karen. She understood now why people said they wanted to pinch themselves to see if they were dreaming. This whole evening was impossible.

Everything had happened just as she'd always hoped. But would Jeff change tomorrow, just as he had at the dance?

She wished she could just relax and trust this happy, contented feeling. After all, she reminded herself, who ever heard of the prince turning back into a frog?

Karen giggled at the thought.

"What is it?" Jeff asked.

She didn't dare tell him what she'd been thinking. Instead, she pointed to a drive-in screen off in the distance down below, on which a man and woman were kissing passionately.

"They're even showing a movie just for us," she whispered.

Jeff nodded and kissed her forehead tenderly. "Maybe it's an omen. Like your cards. Maybe when you told your mom's fortune, you were really telling your own."

Karen sighed and cuddled closer. She wanted this night to last forever.

Chapter Thirteen

Jeff said good-bye at the door and held it open as Karen carried the cat inside.

They looked at each other for a moment, then smiled. His hand squeezed hers lightly, and then he was gone.

They hadn't set a date to see each other again, but why should they? Tomorrow they'd be sitting together in school as usual, only this time their conversations would be warm and affectionate. Everyone would notice the difference: how he complimented her instead of insulting her, how their eyes kept meeting. Elaine would say "I told you so," and Karen wouldn't even mind.

Reluctantly, she started to climb the stairs.

Karen decided to put Garfield in her bedroom, where Doggone couldn't get at him. As she set the cat bed in the corner formerly occupied by Perri's cage, she heard Zack's voice coming from his room

122

and realized he was saying good-bye to someone on the phone.

Tiptoeing into the hall, she glanced through his open door. Zack was lying on the bed staring into space with a wistful expression on his face.

"Talking to Elaine?" she asked, hesitating in the doorway. She was always half-afraid of entering Zack's bedroom for fear of being crushed to death by falling objects. The place was bursting with cheerful clutter, including old-movie posters and oversize film books jammed together precariously on a floor-to-ceiling bookshelf.

"Yeah." He seemed more deliberate than usual, less buoyant. "I'll never understand girls."

"If you did, you could write a book and make a million dollars." Karen edged inside and, moving half a dozen video tapes, sat on a chair.

"You know Elaine pretty well, don't you?" Zack said abruptly. "What's she like?"

"You probably know her better than I do by now," Karen teased.

"How does she feel about me?" Zack asked.

Karen hadn't been prepared for such a blunt question. "Why don't you ask her?"

"I did. She said she likes me a lot, but she won't go out with me because she's already got a boyfriend," Zack explained.

"You can't say you weren't warned." Karen felt bad for her brother, but she sympathized with Elaine, too.

"I think it's just hard for her to break up with Carl," Zack went on, talking half to himself. "He's her first real boyfriend, which makes him special."

"He's also a nice person," Karen reminded him.

"Anyway, I'm certainly not giving up," Zack said, sounding more like his old self. He sat up and flipped open a textbook.

Karen wandered downstairs, thinking about her brother and Elaine. It was hard to see how this situation could work out to suit them both.

She'd never seen Zack act this way over a girl before. He'd always been the happy-go-lucky one in the family. Of course he'd dated a lot, and even had a casual girl friend at college, but none of it had mattered much to him as far as she could tell.

On the other hand, maybe she was reading too much into this. Maybe Zack was just intrigued because Elaine was so hard to get. No, that wasn't likely. Only a shallow guy would act that way, and Zack certainly wasn't shallow.

Hearing the refrigerator door whoosh shut, Karen realized she was hungry. She'd forgotten all about eating dinner in her concern over the cat.

She expected to see Fred in the kitchen, but instead it was Anne who sat at the table. In front of her stood a glass of milk and a whole package of Famous Amos chocolate chip cookies.

Anne never kept cookies in the house. She said she'd swell up like the Goodyear blimp if she did. The only times she went out and bought them were when she was upset or anxious about something.

Had Mr. Becker asked her to marry him? That was the only explanation Karen could think of.

It was even harder to imagine Jeff as her stepbrother now. How could you date somebody who lived in the same house? And yet she couldn't op-

124

pose her mother's happiness, especially now that Karen herself understood what it was like to be in love.

"Hi, Mom," Karen said tentatively. She forced herself to pretend everything was fine as she pulled some bread and peanut butter out of the refrigerator and made herself a sandwich, layering it with a sliced banana. "You missed all the excitement."

She explained about Garfield's accident and how Jeff had come to the rescue.

"Oh, no!" Anne stopped munching on a cookie and stared at her in horror. "I should have been here! That poor cat—I'm glad you were able to reach Art! I'd better go up and have a look."

But something forlorn in her mother's tone made Karen stop her. "You'll only wake him up. You know Art did everything he could. Mom, is something bothering you?"

"Bothering me?" Anne's voice quivered, only a tiny bit, but it vibrated through Karen like a harp.

She set her sandwich on a plate, poured herself some milk, and sat beside her mother. "You only eat cookies when the sky is falling."

Anne laughed nervously. "Am I that transparent? Good heavens, I never realized I could be psycho-analyzed by the food I eat."

"Well?" Karen said.

"Well, you'll be relieved to know that Albert and I aren't going to be seeing much of each other anymore," Anne said, sighing.

Karen felt a rush of emotions, none of them easy to sort out: relief, sure, but also sadness and more than a little guilt.

"I hope it wasn't anything I did," she said.

"Yes and no." Anne washed down a bite of cookie with a sip of milk. "I thought it was so funny, about you and Jeff trying to split us up. Albert had been complaining about how his son was dragging him off to jog and play tennis, and how tired he was getting, and suddenly I realized why."

Karen had to chuckle. "I guess it is pretty funny when you think about it."

Anne nodded. "And here you were, dreaming up problems with French class and ending up spending the evening with Fred reviewing material you probably knew inside and out. I'll bet he figured out exactly what was going on, didn't he?"

"That's right." Karen made a face.

"Anyway, I couldn't resist sharing the joke with Albert," Anne said. "I found out he doesn't have much sense of humor."

"Oops." Karen wondered if Mr. Becker was going to give Jeff a hard time.

"He thought both of you should be punished for interfering," Anne went on. "Of course, I said I thought it was natural for you to be afraid of having your lives disrupted, and that you really didn't do any harm."

"What did he say?"

"He was quite distressed about it. He said that what we do is our business, not yours." Anne sighed again. "We talked for quite a while about our feelings toward children and families, and I discovered we don't have nearly as much in common as I thought we did."

"Oh, Mom." A wave of sadness washed over Karen.

126

"You were having such a good time, and I spoiled it."

"No, honey." Anne reached out and cupped Karen's hand in hers. "I'm old enough to know that moonlight and flowers are fun, but they don't always hold up to the stresses of everyday life. It's much better to find out this early in the relationship that we have such basic differences. Think how much more painful it would have been if we'd gotten serious and then split up."

"I guess that's true," Karen said, but she didn't feel particularly reassured. "On the other hand, we're growing up, the three of us, and in a few years you might want someone to take care of you."

"Take care of me?" Anne's eyes sparkled with humor. "I'm hardly ready for a wheelchair yet."

"But, I mean, you never know." Karen tried to remember exactly what Fred had said, but she couldn't. Suddenly her mother started laughing, and before she knew it Karen was, too. They talked for a little while longer, and Karen helped her mother finish up the cookies.

After flicking out the light on a clean kitchen, hugging her mother good night, and going upstairs to bed, Karen had a sobering thought.

If a romance between two mature grown-ups like her mother and Mr. Becker could dissolve in the space of one conversation, what about her new relationship with Jeff?

She had a feeling his father was going to chew him out about Operation Split. He'd probably think Karen had betrayed him by revealing the plan to her mother.

It was hard to know what was going on in Jeff's

mind. She still didn't really understand why he'd ignored her at that sophomore dance. Okay, so he was afraid of getting rejected; was that a reason to pretend she didn't exist? Or had there been another reason, like that he didn't care enough...?

Karen, trying to fall asleep, kept visualizing one of the tarot cards, the Tower. It showed lightning striking a tower on a fearful night. It meant that something terrible was about to happen.

Chapter Fourteen

As she got ready for school the next day, Karen tried not to worry.

She focused instead on practical things, like deciding to carry her medieval dress in a plastic bag rather than wearing it all day. That way it would be fresh for the fair.

But no matter how practical she tried to be, her mouth was dry, and her heart was pounding with anticipation. Even the thought of breakfast made her positively sick.

Karen didn't see Jeff at the bus stop. Sometimes he got on at the stop on the far side of his house. But she'd hoped he would want to wait with her so they could talk about what had happened with their parents.

Was this a bad sign?

After what seemed like ages, the bus arrived. Karen took a deep breath and climbed up the steps.

Inside, she stood at the front, facing the usual busful of noisy, boisterous kids.

She spotted Jeff at once, and her heart leaped. He was sitting halfway to the back. Beside him on an empty seat was a pile of books.

As the bus started up, Karen grabbed for a handhold and looked at Jeff for a clue as to what she should do next.

But he didn't notice her. He was turned around in his seat, chatting with two of his friends. *Please, Jeff, turn around, notice me,* she prayed as she walked past. But he didn't. Karen's heart crashed. *He knows this is where I always get on,* she thought, *he must be purposely ignoring me.* Was he angry at her for telling her mother about Operation Split? Or was this his way of letting her know he regretted what had happened last night?

Karen's throat tightened. He must have put his books on the seat especially so she wouldn't sit there, even though it was vacant.

A big, hard knot formed in her chest. Everything that had happened between them yesterday, the things they'd talked about, their kisses—didn't they mean anything to Jeff? She had been so sure that he cared as much as she did!

Well, she wasn't going to stand there mooning over him. Fortunately, the other kids didn't seem to have noticed anything strange about her behavior yet.

Stumbling a little as the bus jolted over a pothole, she made her way back to the extralong seat at the rear of the bus where Elaine and Kit were sitting. They scooted over to make room for her.

"Hey, looks like the dress came out great!" Kit laid

part of it in her lap to keep it from wrinkling.

"Thanks. Maybe I'll look like a real fortune-teller." Karen stared glumly down at the dress. She was so upset over Jeff, she couldn't concentrate on anything else.

"Something's bothering you," Elaine said. "What's going on?"

Karen choked back her tears. Much as she liked her new friends, she wasn't ready to tell them about Jeff. The wound was too new and raw; and besides, she couldn't bear it if she burst out crying right there in front of everybody.

Quickly she thought of another explanation. "My mom broke up with Mr. Becker."

"I thought that was what you wanted," Elaine said.

"It was," Karen answered quickly. "But now that it's happened, I don't feel the way I thought I would. I feel bad for her—she was so happy for a while."

The bus halted with a squeal of brakes, jostling them all together, and three freshman boys climbed aboard. Jeff leaned forward to greet them, his back still turned to Karen, as if he hadn't noticed her—or didn't want to.

"Why did she do it?" Kit asked. "It wasn't your fault, I'm sure."

"Oh, she and Mr. Becker found out they didn't have as much in common as they thought." Karen left her answer vague. After all, her mother probably wouldn't appreciate having details of her personal life gossiped about on the bus where anyone might hear.

"Talk about having things in common"—Kit shot

Elaine a knowing look—"your phone was busy for two hours last night. I guess you and Zack haven't run out of things to talk about yet."

Elaine groaned. "I don't know what I'm going to do."

"Have you told Carl?" Kit probed.

"That I'm spending all my spare time on the phone with another guy?" Elaine shook her head. "I don't know how he'd react. I don't think he'd get mad —I can't picture Carl turning out to be the macho type—but he'd probably feel hurt."

Karen bit her lip, trying to concentrate on Elaine's problems but unable to stop thinking about Jeff.

Was this what love felt like? Her rib cage ached, and her lungs squeezed together so tightly she could hardly breathe. In movies and books, people usually fell in love with people who loved them back. Why had she picked the wrong guy?

The rest of the day was a struggle to get through. Jeff hardly seemed aware that Karen existed. At least he didn't tease her, she told herself, but that wasn't much consolation.

At lunch, she ate out on the lawn with Elaine and Lori. Jeff was sitting not far away with some of his friends. From the snatches of conversation she overheard, Karen could tell they were discussing the fair and how the video games booth would look. She couldn't believe his insensitivity!

"Are you worried about the fair?" Lori asked sympathetically. "You seem kind of tense."

Karen nodded, grateful that her friend had misinterpreted her gloomy expression. "I wish I'd never agreed to do this, but I want to help that little boy."

"We're planning to come," Elaine volunteered. "I keep hoping next time the cards will give me a clue what to do."

I wish some fortune-teller would tell me what to do, Karen thought, seething with angry frustration. But with her friends' support, she managed to wrench her mind away from Jeff for at least five minutes before it was time to return to class.

Last period, the Social Services Committee members were excused early from their classes so they could set up the fair. They had decided to use the quad because of its central location. Hurrying outside with her fortune-telling paraphernalia, Karen saw that many of the students, as she had, had built wooden booths and made signs. She stared at her own with pride. It read: MADAME WAVERLY, SEES ALL, KNOWS ALL, YOUR FORTUNE, ONLY $1.

For her booth Ms. O'Neill had provided her with a shower curtain rod shaped in a U and hung with old paisley Indian bedspreads.

Karen had to climb up on a ladder to attach it to the wall with built-in suction cups. Struggling awkwardly with the rod, she looked around for help.

Jeff was talking animatedly with Christina Farrel across the quad. He seemed oblivious of Karen. Just looking at his lean, familiar figure in a new dark-blue sweater made Karen's chest start to ache again. Only yesterday he'd held her in his arms, and already he'd changed his mind. If only she could change her heart as easily!

"Need some help?" It was Ben Davidson.

"Oh, sure. Thanks." Karen climbed down, trying not to show how upset she was.

133

While Ben finished attaching the rod, she dragged a small table and two chairs into her makeshift booth and then went to change into her Gypsy dress in the girls' bathroom.

Standing in front of the mirror, she hardly recognized herself. Wow, the dress really looked great on her! Lori had certainly been right about the color. Russet went perfectly with her hair.

Maybe this was the start of a new Karen. All the guys would notice how terrific she looked. They'd clamor around her asking for dates, and by the end of the day she'd hardly remember Jeff existed.

Yeah, sure, she thought, her brief hopefulness turning to despair as she remembered the way Jeff had ignored her.

Although the last class wasn't over yet, kids were already circulating around Jeff's computer monitors by the time she got back to the quad. Several couples were pestering Ms. O'Neill to find out when the dance contest would start.

Karen slipped behind her curtain and drew out her cards, shuffling them to keep busy. Her hands felt prickly.

The clanging of the last bell made her jump. It was followed by shouts, pounding feet, and the slam of lockers as the students raced out to the fair.

The first two people to want their fortunes told were Roseanne Parker and Barry Gordon.

Barry was on crutches because of a pole-vaulting accident earlier that year. Roseanne, a cheerleader and star of the Drama Club, had gone through some hard times adjusting to her boyfriend's accident, but now the couple was closer than ever.

They sat together while she did a reading for each one. Fortunately, the cards came out positively, although they showed the need for a lot of strength and contending against odds.

"As long as I have Roseanne beside me, I can take anything," Barry announced, lifting Roseanne's hand in his and smiling at her tenderly. They were so much in love, Karen thought with a pang. Why couldn't Jeff care about her the way Barry did about Roseanne?

Lori, Elaine, Alex, and Kit all came in just as they'd promised. Their cards showed a fairly normal jumble of good and bad events.

As soon as they left, a bunch of underclassmen lined up in front of the booth. They giggled and poked each other and, through the curtains, Karen could hear them daring each other to go in.

One of the boys stuck his nose through the curtains. "Is this gonna be a funny fortune?"

"That depends on whether you've got a funny future," Karen shot back.

Some of the boys came in, and a lot of younger girls, including Andrea. She got very excited when the Two of Cups turned up, showing a boy and girl toasting each other. Karen obviously made her afternoon when she told Andrea she might soon have a boyfriend.

It wasn't until the dance contest started that Karen finally got a chance to quit. Her booth had been one of the most popular at the fair! *If only I was in demand as much as my fortune-telling services,* she thought ruefully.

Karen stepped outside, drawn to the beat of the

music. She watched the dancers gyrating as the judges, Cheryl Abrahamson, the head cheerleader, and Steve Milner, her current boyfriend and the Wildcat quarterback, walked among the crowd to select the finalists.

One sophomore boy was practically lying flat on the ground, wiggling, while his partner shuffled her feet nearby. Cheryl tapped the girl's shoulder, which meant they were out. The girl hurried away, looking almost grateful the ordeal was over, while the boy went on thrashing for a few seconds before he realized what had happened.

Through the crowd of dancers, Karen saw Justin lift Kit overhead. She was poised gracefully, arms outstretched, toes pointed. When he lowered her, she landed perfectly, not missing a beat of the music. You could see she was serious about her dancing and not just some kid fooling around.

By the time the music ended, there was just one couple left: Kit and Justin. Everyone cheered, and Karen and Elaine, who'd come to stand beside her, clapped until their hands hurt. Ms. O'Neill presented the winning couple with a pair of movie tickets and a bouquet of roses.

As the crowd began to break up, Karen glanced over at Jeff. He was standing in the middle of a group of admiring younger girls who were taking turns flirting with him under the pretense of asking questions about video games.

Jeff glanced up and, for the first time all day, he finally seemed to notice her. "Hey, Karen!" he called. "Come over here!"

Since people were watching, she couldn't very well

pretend she hadn't heard. Her heart pounding, Karen dragged herself across the quad.

Jeff's eyes grew wide as Karen approached. For a moment, Karen allowed herself to believe that he was actually going to say something nice about her new dress. "That dress makes you look like something out of the Middle Ages," Jeff said with a grin. "You're not exactly what I'd call middle-aged!"

Everybody laughed but Karen.

It was her turn. From around the video booth, faces watched expectantly. Everyone was waiting for Karen to say something funny, the way she always did.

Only she couldn't. Her mind had gone blank. The only thing she could think about was that Jeff was making a point of showing her, in front of everybody, that he didn't care one bit how she felt. Her throat clamped shut. Karen couldn't have uttered a word even if she'd thought of something clever to say — and she did not.

Feeling the blood rise to her cheeks, she whirled around, snatched up her tarot cards, and dashed out of the courtyard.

Elaine and Alex caught up with her in the bathroom. Karen hated to have them see her cry, but she couldn't help it. Tears streamed down her cheeks.

A younger girl started to come in after them, but Alex shooed her away. "This is private," she said. "Go use the one down the hall."

Her friends' concern only made Karen cry harder.

"It's okay." Elaine glanced approvingly at Alex, who was standing guard at the door. "Nobody'll come in here. Let it all out."

"I can't stand him!" Karen wailed. "I hate him!" She knew she was behaving like a three-year-old, but it *did* feel good to let it all out.

"You really like him, don't you?" Elaine hadn't been fooled for a minute. "Why can't he see it? The dumb ox." She pulled a wad of tissues out of her purse. Trust Elaine to be prepared for anything, Karen thought, as she blew her nose.

Finally, after washing her face three times with cold water and daubing on some powder and lipstick, she looked marginally human again.

"Tell me what you need from your locker, and I'll get it," Alex said. "Then we'll drive you home."

"Lori and Kit are taking your booth apart," Elaine added. "They'll make sure everything's squared away with Ms. O'Neill, so don't worry."

Gratefully, Karen accepted their help, especially the way they hustled her out like secret service agents guarding the president. The last thing she wanted to do was to see Jeff Becker again.

Ever.

Chapter Fifteen

Maybe the tears set it off, or maybe it was just chance, but Karen came down with a honking bad cold and had to stay home from school for the next two days.

Trying to concentrate on Zack's collection of old movies, which he'd generously put at her disposal, she found herself instead replaying over in her mind the scene at the fair. Every time she did, Karen hurt all over again.

The only sign that Jeff remembered her existence was a jarful of azalea blossoms he left at the door on Tuesday afternoon. They were pretty and cheerful, but they probably had a potato bug in them if you looked hard enough — but Karen hadn't. She'd thrown them out, not wanting to have anything in the house that reminded her of Jeff.

Ms. O'Neill telephoned Tuesday evening to say the fair had raised almost $250. A group of policemen had donated some more money, and now the little boy's family had enough to go ahead with his heart operation. Karen was glad she'd been able to help, but somehow even that good news did little to alleviate her depression.

Garfield, however, was making a splendid recovery. He kept Karen company and by Wednesday was hobbling around her bedroom, clearly annoyed by the restricting splints and bandages.

She felt almost grateful for her illness. She'd needed the time to pull herself together so she could face everybody.

By Wednesday night, Karen decided she felt well enough to go to the gathering at Elaine's. She wasn't sneezing anymore, and Anne agreed that she probably wasn't contagious. But she still hadn't gotten over Jeff. How long does it take for a broken heart to heal? she wondered.

Zack insisted on driving her over. At the Gregorys', he waited while Karen went up and rang the doorbell, and he looked disappointed when Andrea answered it instead of Elaine.

But he didn't seem too discouraged. "Give me a call when you're ready to come home!" he shouted before driving off.

Everyone else had already arrived. Elaine's narrow room was crowded with five girls sitting in it, yet the feeling was congenial rather than cramped.

"Hey, we didn't know if you could come!" Alex squeezed over on the bed and cleared room for Karen.

Kit and Lori were there, too, along with Alex's foster sister, Stephanie. They all greeted Karen warmly.

"Listen, everybody, thanks for your help on Monday," she said. "I don't know what I'd have done without you."

"Hey, we were glad we could help." Alex handed her a bag of potato chips, and Karen took a couple before passing it on.

"You didn't happen to bring your cards tonight, did you?" Stephanie asked. "Rick and I were in the dance contest, and I missed the fortune-telling."

Karen nibbled on one of the chips. "I've given up on the tarot. You can't trust it, or at least not when I'm doing the reading," she explained. "My mother's fortune showed true love ahead, and instead she and her boyfriend broke up."

"Have you heard anything from Jeff?" Elaine asked. "I thought maybe he'd call and apologize."

"He left a bunch of azaleas on the front porch, but I'm sure it doesn't mean anything. I...I guess I should try and explain to you guys why I got so upset," Karen said. She took a deep breath and spilled out the whole story of what had happened Sunday evening after Garfield was hurt.

"He's a strange guy," Stephanie commented.

"Strange? Somebody ought to pound some sense into his thick head!" Alex declared, ripping open a fresh bag of potato chips for emphasis.

"It's awful, having a crush on a guy who doesn't feel the same way," Elaine said. "Remember Rusty? I made a fool of myself before I figured out there was as much padding in his head as on his shoulders."

"I don't understand why Jeff would lead her on that way," Kit added. "It's really cruel. He never struck me as the mean type before, but I guess you never know, do you?"

Karen immediately began to feel better. Having a whole group of friends who sympathized with her—even if they couldn't solve her problem—made her feel strong.

"I can't understand why he'd want to hurt you." Lori was sitting cross-legged on the floor. "You must feel terrible. Anyone can see you're a sensitive person."

"They can?" Karen asked. "I thought people saw me as kind of a buffoon. You know, punch her button and she says something clever."

"Maybe if they don't know you well," Elaine agreed, "but after we spent some time together, it was obvious that underneath you were really shy."

Karen stared at her in amazement. "You could tell that?"

Heads nodded agreement around the room.

Karen couldn't believe it. These girls had seen right through her defenses. And they liked her anyway! She felt as if a burden had been lifted from her shoulders.

"Did I make a fool of myself at the fair?" she asked. "I felt like such an idiot, standing there staring at Jeff, but I couldn't think of anything to say."

"He was the one who looked like a fool," Kit said.

"I'm afraid that's what I'm going to be like when I meet my mother," Stephanie muttered. "I won't be able to get a word out."

"You'll do great," Alex told her foster sister loyally. "Your mom will love you."

"Rick thinks finding my mother is a terrible idea," Stephanie admitted. "He doesn't understand what it's like to grow up without a family. Sometimes we argue about it."

"I guess it is hard for people who've always had a home to put themselves in your place," Elaine said thoughtfully. "I take it for granted that I've got three sisters and two parents."

"What *is* it like, Stephanie?" Karen asked. "I can understand that you'd be curious about your mother, but after all, you've got people here who love you."

Stephanie, who was sitting on the rug by the door, picked some lint off one of her tennis shoes. "I don't want to leave here. That isn't the idea."

"I certainly hope not!" Alex huffed.

"It's part of finding out who you are, isn't it?" Lori suggested. Her eyes were large, and it looked almost as if she were going to cry. Karen knew that Lori lived with her mother because her father was an alcoholic. Perhaps she was thinking about him now.

"That's right," Stephanie said. "All kinds of things are involved. Like, do I have other relatives, grandparents and aunts and uncles and cousins? What's my family's medical history? Just think, someday I might need a bone marrow transplant or something, and I wouldn't even know where to start looking."

Karen tried to put herself in Stephanie's position. "I guess you don't even know why your mom left, do you?"

"That's right." Stephanie looked down at her lap, avoiding their eyes. "It's like there's this great big blank in my past. It's hard to figure out where you're going when you don't know where you've come from."

143

Karen thought about her own father. At least she'd had the chance to spend nine whole years with him. And even now, she still had the rest of her family.

The conversation turned to college and careers. Before they knew it, Elaine's mother trotted up the stairs to remind them it was after ten o'clock on a school night. Karen couldn't believe the time had gone so fast.

Everyone was spilling outside when Zack arrived. Amid the loud good-byes and waves, Karen noted how Elaine and Zack's eyes met, although neither of them said anything.

Leaning her head back against the seat as she rode home silently with Zack, Karen remembered how wonderful she'd felt with Jeff. For a few hours, they'd had the perfect relationship.

And now it was all over. Jeff had turned away as easily as he'd turned to Meredith Shaw two years ago.

How could he have given her that glimpse of happiness, only to snatch it away? Hadn't he enjoyed their time together, too?

She could never understand him, not if she lived a million years, she thought, the wound inside her opening up again, making her wish she'd never met Jeff Becker—much less fallen in love with him.

Chapter Sixteen

Karen sneezed as she picked up the stack of files.
"I thought you were over that cold." Art had come
out of the surgery room to take the next client, a furry gray kitten whose cage was clutched by a worried
little boy.

"I am." She set the files on the desk. "I think I'm al-
lergic to this office."

"Well, don't work too hard. Two Saturdays in a row
is a lot for a popular girl like you to give up," Art
teased.

Karen smiled, but she felt as though her lips would
crack from the effort. "Somehow I managed to tear
myself away from my admirers."

As the veterinarian escorted the little boy and the
kitten to the back room, she looked glumly around
the waiting area.

The only patient left was a Siamese cat sitting on
the lap of a thin-faced woman. Both the woman and

the cat wore the same disdainful expression.

Anne often said that pets and their owners tended to resemble each other. Do I look like Garfield? Karen wondered, smiling to herself as she pictured the furry orange cat and thought of her own hair. Yes, there was definitely a resemblance.

She turned back to her work. She'd been there since ten o'clock, almost six hours, and in that time had made only a few inroads into the accumulated papers.

A secretary had been hired to start Monday, and the last thing Karen wanted was for her to take one look at the mess and quit in disgust.

Anne had planned to help with the paperwork between clients, but she'd had to go out to a farm to deliver a colt. She'd invited Karen to go along, and that had sounded like a lot more fun than working in this stuffy office! But Karen couldn't shirk her responsibility.

The front door swung open amid the tinkling of bells. Karen looked up.

Bluto the retriever came through the door first. Then Jeff stepped inside.

The sight of him hit her like a blow. They'd been avoiding each other at school these last two days. Why did he have to bring his dog in now? He really had a lot of nerve! All the feelings of hurt and anger she'd been struggling to put behind her came welling to the suface.

Jeff walked up to the desk. "We're not too late, are we?" he asked stiffly. "I promised Dad I'd bring Bluto over to make sure his wounds healed okay."

He gave her a long look, but from his impersonal

one, he might have been talking to some girl he'd never seen before.

Karen's cheeks burned, but she would have died rather than let him know how upset she was. "We're open until five," she said in her coolest, most professional voice. "If you'll have a seat, you'll be next after this lady here."

"Okay." He strolled to a seat, pulling lightly on the retriever's leash to make him follow. He didn't look back or even say "Bless you" when Karen sneezed again from the dust.

She wanted to kick him.

She was also acutely aware of how dirty she must be. She probably had smudge marks on her cheeks from the dusty files, and her hair was held back with an old headband. Since the work was so dirty, she'd worn faded jeans and a gray sweat shirt.

On the other hand, Jeff looked wonderful in a tan polo shirt and brown cords. Why did he have to be so infuriatingly handsome?

Maybe he had a date tonight and wasn't sure he'd have time to change after he got home. Karen's eyes stung just thinking about it. Maybe he was going out with Sherri Cunningham or one of the younger girls who'd flocked around him at the fair.

Trying to ignore him, she moved a couple of more stacks of files onto the desk and busied herself looking through them.

An angry hissing sound made her look up. The Siamese cat was glaring at Bluto. Although Jeff had sat on the opposite side of the room, the space was small and the animals were in dangerously close proximity, Karen realized.

"Maybe it would be better if you waited outside," she started to say, but her words came too late.

With a lunge, Bluto snapped forward, jerking his leash out of Jeff's hands.

The cat yowled and arched, swelling up to twice its size. Karen could see that its claws were unsheathed and digging into its mistress's arm. She winced in sympathy.

"Get that dog out of here!" the woman shouted as Bluto leaped.

Jeff flung himself toward his dog but stumbled. The cat shot out of its owner's arms with the dog in pursuit, and Jeff landed on the woman's lap.

Everything happened at once in a blur of movement—like a Saturday morning cartoon. Karen grabbed for Bluto's leash but missed. Apologizing profusely, Jeff stood up, then tripped again, his foot caught in the leash, and fell sprawled on the floor. His face had turned a fiery shade of red that Karen—irrelevantly remembering a box of crayons she'd once owned—decided could best be described as vermillion.

Screeching, the cat tried to climb up a pole lamp, then turned to rake its claws across Bluto's nose.

With a yelp, the retriever scooted backwards, and there was a momentary standoff.

"Bluto!" Having finally disentangled himself, Jeff stalked firmly toward his pet.

Everything might have settled down then if a stray draft hadn't sent another particle of dust swirling into Karen's nose.

She sneezed loudly. The Siamese, its nerves on edge, jumped like a shot, landing on the desk. It tried to run, but the papers spewed out from under its feet, so that for a moment, the cat looked as if it were racing in place, lost in a blizzard of white.

Galvanized into action, Bluto gathered himself on his hind quarters and sprang. His front paws caught another stack of files on top of the desk, and, barking frantically, he pulled them over the edge.

Jeff grabbed Bluto. The woman grabbed the cat. At the same moment, the inner door opened to reveal Art and the little boy, who stood gaping in the doorway.

The woman thrust past them, carrying the cat into the surgery. The kitten, which looked very much like Perri with its soft gray fur, uttered a thin, high-pitched meow.

"What on earth is going on?" Art said. "Was anybody hurt?"

Jeff, hanging on tightly to the leash of the now-docile Bluto, shook his head. "Just my pride. I'm really sorry, Dr. Brenner. My dog caused all the trouble."

Karen gazed in dismay at the papers scattered around the floor. "My whole day's work!"

"I'll help get things straightened out," Jeff promised.

"Oh . . . just forget it!" Karen glared at him. The idea of spending the rest of the day with Jeff was worse than the prospect of sorting out all the papers herself.

"I'll put Bluto in the back room, in case any more cats come in," Art suggested, "I'll look at him as soon as I can."

Watching the dog pad quietly beside the veterinarian, Karen found it hard to believe Bluto was responsible for this mess. The room looked as if a tornado had hit it.

Now she really wanted to cry.

A heavy silence hung in the air, thicker than the dust. The only noise was the rustle of papers as Jeff began collecting them.

Karen couldn't stand it anymore. "Look, why don't you just leave," she choked, dangerously close to bursting into tears. "I can do this myself."

"I said I'd help," Jeff muttered.

"Forget it, just forget it!" She shoved her slipping headband furiously back into place, heedless of the dirt she was probably smearing across her forehead. "I don't need anything from you, Jeff Becker. And the next time you want to make a fool of somebody, go pick on someone else."

He stared at her. "I don't know what you're talking about."

Tears were running down her face now, and she angrily brushed them away. "Just stop it, Jeff. No more teasing. I don't want any more of your games. If you're not interested in me, just say so, instead of pretending to be so you can laugh about it later on!

"Oh, I know, you must think I'm the biggest f-fool in the wah-wah-world." Karen was sobbing openly now. "Not only was I stupid enough to like you s-sophomore year, I fell for you again even though I knew better. I actually b-believed all that stuff you said on Sunday!"

"I did mean it!" Jeff jumped to his feet, his voice echoing through the room. "You're the one who changed your mind!" He started toward her.

Karen stopped crying and simply stared at him. "*Me*? *You're* the one who ignored me on the bus. You even put your books on that seat so I wouldn't sit there."

He circled the desk, and she backed away, feeling so vulnerable, like a piece of fragile glass that might shatter if he touched her.

But she didn't break when he put his arms around her. Instead she felt as if she were melting.

"Now will you listen to me?" he murmured close to her ear.

Karen made a halfhearted attempt to pull back, but his arms were wrapped so tightly around her, she couldn't. "It doesn't look like I have much choice."

"Now" — Jeff's voice echoed all the way down her bones — "I did save that seat for you. That's why I put the books there in the first place."

Karen stood, her heart fluttering. Could she believe him this time? Was it true?

"I couldn't figure out why you ignored me all day Monday." He nuzzled her ear tenderly. Shivery sensations ran up and down Karen's spine. "You kept avoiding me, and then you were shut up in that booth telling fortunes, so I didn't get to talk to you until you came out. I didn't want to make a big scene about how you'd been acting, so I thought I'd kid you out of it."

"Some kidding!" She tried to sound angry, but the warmth of Jeff's arms around her was making it hard.

"I didn't mean it as an insult. It just came out that way." Jeff sounded regretful. "Somehow I always get

151

off on the wrong foot with you."

"Today, it was the wrong *paw*," she retorted.

"Karen, I really do care about you." He released her but kept hold of her hand. "I'm sorry I've been so clumsy, the way I've gone around trying to get your attention. Even when I try to do things right, I seem to screw up."

Hope swelled inside her, like a balloon threatening to lift her right off her feet. "What do you mean?"

"Well, like the flowers." He brushed a tear from her face with his hand. "I remembered the azaleas in the park, and I thought it would be kind of romantic to send you some. That day when we played on the swings and talked about our parents, that was special to me."

"I—I never thought of that," she admitted.

"I guess I should have come right out a long time ago and told you how much I liked you, but I thought you'd laugh." Jeff gazed at her wistfully. "I figured you'd give me the brush-off, so the only way I could get near you was to goof around. Only that's not good enough anymore. Forgive me?"

"Oh, Jeff." Karen couldn't resist reaching out and touching his cheek lightly. "I thought—I mean, I interpreted everything—well... You sure are hard to figure out."

They bent toward each other, almost kissing—and then sprang apart as the door opened and Art came out with Bluto. The lady and the cat must have gone out the side door, Karen realized with relief.

"Your dog looks just fine," Art said.

"Thanks. Well, I guess we'd better finish cleaning up," Jeff said gruffly.

Somehow straightening up with Jeff's help wasn't nearly as hard as it had been by herself, Karen discovered. It was amazing how often they stumbled against each other, brushed hands, or just stopped and looked at each other longingly.

Finally he caught her up in his arms for a long kiss that jolted Karen down to her toes. Jeff smelled like dust and after-shave—absolutely wonderful.

By five o'clock, they'd managed to restore enough order not to frighten off the new secretary.

They dropped Bluto off at Jeff's house and then drove to the park, where they headed for the swings and sat there side by side.

The park was quiet for a Saturday afternoon. Everyone must be inside having dinner, Karen decided. She felt more peaceful than she had in years.

"Maybe we could start over," Jeff said, rocking his swing lightly. Karen kept pace, and they swung back and forth in a slow rhythm.

"Back to the second grade?" she asked.

He laughed. "We kind of got stuck there, didn't we? You know, I guess I was afraid that if we ever got close, you'd leave the way my mother did. It was safer to keep you as a friend, somebody to goof around with. Isn't that ironic? I was trying to hold on to you, yet what I really did was nearly drive you away."

"I guess we were both afraid of getting hurt, so we were trying to protect ourselves," Karen said. "Trying to pretend we didn't really care much."

"I care a lot." Jeff's gaze met hers straight-on.

"So do I." Karen's throat clenched. She didn't have any disguises left. But then she realized she didn't need any.

"Boy, will everybody at school be surprised," Jeff said. "Maybe we could tell them we got picked up by a flying saucer and when we got off, we found they'd made us fall in love."

"Maybe we could just tell the truth," Karen answered, "that we discovered we've been in love all along."

The words scared her a little. She peered sideways at Jeff, half-afraid of his reaction. But he was grinning. Her heart swelled with happiness.

"Now I can take you out on dates, like I've always wanted," Jeff announced, clearly pleased by the change in their status. "And we can sit together at lunch and on the school bus..." He paused, then took her hand and added, "You're my best friend, Karen."

"And you're mine," she answered, feeling warm and comfortable and at home.

By unspoken agreement, they began to swing hand in hand, arcing back and forth, going higher and higher. But this time they weren't competing; they were helping each other.

"The sky's the limit," Karen called, and they both laughed, his deep voice and her softer one floating out together into the evening breeze.